THE DOG, RAY

THE DOG, RAY

Linda Coggin

CANDLEWICK PRESS

Copyright © 2015 by Linda Coggin

First U.S. edition 2016

Library of Congress Catalog Card Number pending
ISBN 978-0-7636-7938-5

16 17 18 19 20 21 BVG 10 9 8 7 6 5 4 3 2 1

Printed in Berryville, VA, U.S.A.

This book was typeset in Sabon.

Candlewick Press
99 Dover Street
Somerville, Massachusetts 02144

visit us at www.candlewick.com

For Chloë

Chapter 1

When my death came it was swift. Swift as a running horse. It wasted no time. Like a magic trick. One moment I was in the car, the next on the road, and then I wasn't anywhere. When I awoke I was slouched in a chair in a room with yellow paint peeling off the walls and a table at the far end. Yes. My death was as fleet as the wind. Meteoric, you might say. Mercurial, like quicksilver. No floating above the body, looking down on the grieving relatives. It was snappy, prompt. It was *fast*.

It's funny, now that I think of it. My dad, who was driving the car, always did have a fear of horses. He was so afraid of them he would never get on one, or pat one on the neck, or let their lovely soft muzzles blow in his face. I know all this because my mom had told me how scared of horses he was.

"It's unreasonable, really," she'd said. "He's never had anything to do with them. It's not like he was kicked by one when he was small."

And that *is* what's funny. Because the reason I ended up on the road was because a horse jumped over a hedge and onto my dad's car as we were driving to the supermarket. So it had been a premonition. His fear of horses.

"You'd better hurry up, dear," said someone at the table at the far end of the room, "or all the best jobs will be taken. We had a multiple-bus crash just before you came in, and most of the qualified jobs are gone."

"Jobs?" I asked. "Why do I need a job? I'm only twelve."

"*Were* only twelve, dear," the voice corrected.

"I've got you down as Daisy Fellows. Distinguishing features one blue eye and one green eye. Is that right?"

I nodded. I had always longed to have one of those old-fashioned passports that Mom had told me about. I'd never seen one, but Mom said they used to have a section for distinguishing marks. I thought whoever read it would have to look long into my eyes to make sure it was true, and I would learn to perfect a blank stare so that they wouldn't be able to see into my soul. But they don't do that anymore. The passport I got last year just had a little microchip in it that probably said everything there is to know about me, including my bad grade on the math exam.

A woman was sorting out a pile of papers on the desk and she glanced at me every now and then.

"Really, my dear, you must go while you can. A new baby is about to be born in Springfield. It's the only qualified job left. I think we've got about two minutes, so come and sign the form and then you must go."

"Go? I don't understand," I said. "I've only

just arrived. And I don't even know where I am. Is this Heaven or something?"

"Heaven? Goodness, my dear. What an old-fashioned concept of death. You are in one of our Job Centers. You are a *soul,* are you not? Everyone who is born needs a soul. It's just a question of whose body you take up. Look at it as rehousing."

She was just about to hand me a form to sign when a telephone rang at her side. She picked it up.

"Oh, dear. Well, thank you for letting me know." The woman looked at me. "The job was taken. We'll have to find you something else."

"Why is no one else here?" I asked. "Six thousand three hundred and ninety people die per hour. I learned that in school. Where are they all?"

"That's an old figure, my dear. Far more people die than that. But that's not the point. The point is we like to treat people as *individuals.* There are lots of rooms in the building, you know, and lines of people waiting to come in here."

"What about my dad? He's here, isn't he?"

"I don't know, dear — what's his name?"

"Dennis Fellows."

The woman opened a drawer marked *F* and rifled through it. "Fanshawe. Featherstone. Fielding. No Dennis Fellows; there's a Freddie Fellows — any relation?"

I shook my head.

"He's not dead, then," she said.

Good, I thought. *Mom'll be pleased. And no joint funeral. Thank goodness. I wouldn't want to be buried to something by the Beatles.* I thought about it for a moment. It would've been fun to see who'd come to it — most of the seventh grade, I guess. I hoped Owen Taylor showed up and cried buckets for me. Of course, technically I wouldn't have had my funeral yet. I was probably still lying on the road, covered in a sheet. I bet there was a crowd of people. They always stop and stare at accidents. I wondered what had happened to the horse. Perhaps it was in the line outside, waiting to come back as a hedgehog.

"So Mom was right about her theory of coming back again as something else when you die?" I said. "She was into Buddhism."

"It's not about *religion*," the woman said scornfully. "It's about practicalities. Now you're getting cold, aren't you? I can see you shivering. We must hurry. Ah, yes. You needn't sign any forms for this one — it's not a qualified job. Off you go, dear — through that door on the right."

"But what's my — uh . . . who, uh — *what's my job? Who will I become?*"

"There's a litter being born right now in a charming house. I'm sure you'll like it. They're nearly all out, but I'll arrange for one to be stuck in the birth canal. That'll give you about three minutes to get there. Remember — *the door on the right!*"

I just had the handle in my hand when the door flew open. It definitely seemed like sky out there, and when I looked down, a jagged vent opened up and it felt as if something had grabbed hold of my legs. Too late, I realized — I had gone through the door on the left. Out of the corner of my eye I'd seen a sign — ABSOLUTELY NO EXIT.

I was supposed to go through *the door on the right*. I found myself falling, falling. And it was as quick as the wind. It was snappy, prompt. It was *fast*.

As I fell I remember shouting out, "What sort of litter? Am I going to be a pig? A cat? *A rat?*" But no one heard me, and it wasn't until I could open my eyes twelve days later that I could see, perfectly well, that I had come back to Earth as a dog.

Chapter 2

"So which of these dear little puppies would you like, Cyril?" the woman in the alarmingly pink dress asks.

"Me! Me! Take me!" they all say, their little tails wagging.

Why? Who would want to go with a woman in a pink dress? I could just imagine her home. It would probably have pink furry seat covers on the toilets.

I hide under the table.

Cyril picks up one of my brothers by the tail, and he gives a loud yelp.

"Cyril! Don't do that. Now, which one do you want?"

"Me! Me! Take me!" they all go again, jumping up and making themselves appear as adorable as possible.

"I want that one hiding under the table," he says, getting down on his hands and knees and peering at me. I glare at him. He smells like candy and socks.

"Urgh—look, Mom! It's got funny eyes. They're different colors. I don't want it after all."

"I don't know, Cyril," the woman says, looking under the table. "It's rather sweet. Anyway, it's the only female. And I did say we'd get a girl. I don't want some boy dog running after everything that moves."

Cyril lets out a wail. "Don't want a girl. Want a boy to play soccer with."

I growl at him.

"Cyril, it's just a *dog.* I'm sure you can throw a ball for it, but it won't be able to play soccer."

"Actually, I *can* play soccer," I tell them. "I was on the JV soccer team at my school. I've scored literally *hundreds* of goals." But they don't understand me.

"Oh, look, the poor thing is *whimpering*. My mind is made up, Cyril. It's adorable."

I never do get to see if they have pink furry covers on the toilets because when they get me back they proudly show me my new home. A doghouse — outside!

"I'm not sleeping in *that*," I say. "I want a basket, at least. And perhaps one of those nice plaid rugs or, even better, a *beanbag*. Now *that* would be comfy. I imagine I'll be doing a lot of lying around. I'm sure they wouldn't have let you take me if they'd known I was going to have to sleep *outside*!"

"I think she likes it," the woman in the pink dress says. "Come on, Cyril, we must leave her to rest. We'll come back and see her later."

"Rest?" I say. "I'm not an invalid!"

"I want to play soccer," Cyril whines.

"So do I!"

"All in due course, Cyril. Lunchtime first. Spaghetti and meatballs."

"I love spaghetti and meatballs," I say, and jump up and down to get some attention. "It's practically my favorite food—after Thai green curry."

"I think she's telling us she needs to go pee-pee," Cyril's mother says. "Go on, Cyril, go and put her on the newspaper in the yard and then we must go in and have our lunch."

Cyril grabs me by the neck and drags me, protesting, to the yard. Cyril's house looks much like everyone else's on the road. It has a neat square of grass, a garage with double doors, and a little concrete area on which his mother has placed some pages from a newspaper. Dragging my heels, I reluctantly follow him. My mom always advised me to take any opportunity I could to use a bathroom. "Because you just don't know when or where you'll get another chance."

As I stand over the paper my eye catches sight of the headline.

GIRL AND HORSE KILLED IN FATAL ROAD ACCIDENT. MAN LEFT PARALYZED. And there, smiling back at me, is my picture.

What on earth possessed them to use that picture? It's my school photo. I look demented and about six years old. Why couldn't they have used that one taken on the beach in Turkey? The one with my hair looking particularly good—kind of windswept and interesting.

There is another picture of a mass of flowers and teddy bears that *"friends of Daisy have left at the spot where she was killed."* I look at the date on the paper and see that it is about three months old. I've already been a dog for a quarter of a year.

After I recover from the thought of my school photo being seen by thousands of readers, I think of my poor dad being paralyzed. I wonder how he and Mom are coping. I look back at the paper again. How could I possibly pee on *that*?

I am lying here. Waiting. Waiting to hear someone call my name. *Misty!* What sort of silly name is *that*? I don't look like a Misty. I caught a glimpse of myself in the reflection of a puddle the other day. I've got sharp features. A long pointy nose and funny little ears that flop over at the top. But I can make them stand up when I feel like it, which is really cool.

So here I am, *waiting*. Waiting for someone to take me for a walk. I would take myself for a walk, but I'm attached to this doghouse. Not like I'm fond of it. I'm attached with a cord. And Cyril cannot be relied upon to take me for a decent walk. His mother bribes him to take me for a walk twice a day, in the park, because she feels he "needs the exercise." Looking at him, I think she's right.

He goes around the corner all right, but once out of sight he either sits on a bench and plays with his phone or doubles back when he thinks his mother isn't looking. Then he hides me in the garage while he sneaks into the kitchen and takes a snack from the cookie jar. And he never gives *me* a cookie. When I get a biscuit it is in the shape of a bone. Who are they trying to kid? Are they trying to fool me into thinking it's a bone? A bone doesn't look like that—a bone doesn't *smell* like that. And, even worse, when he *does* give me a biscuit — uh, bone — he expects me to turn into a circus act before he'll let me have it. Now, if it were Thai green curry, for example, I'd sit down, beg, roll over — I'd do a cartwheel if I could — but it isn't. It's a boring bone-biscuit.

In fact, I know I should like Cyril, in a dog way, but I can't help worrying that he's going to do something nasty to me. He doesn't seem to realize that I'm not a toy and that I have feelings, like he does. I remember Mr. Pearce talking about the Second World War and how the Russians trained their dogs to run suicide missions with mines strapped to their backs. I hope Cyril hasn't studied the Second World War yet, because I think it might put ideas into his head.

He doesn't seem to have any friends, never talks to me, and seems almost incapable of laughing. The only time I saw Cyril laugh was when he gave me some bubblegum and my teeth got stuck together. It was humiliating, because I've had a lot of bubblegum in my time and I used to be able to blow the biggest bubbles in the whole school. But the new jaws I've got don't work quite the same way. I thought it was mean of him to laugh like that. I don't think that strapping a mine onto my back can be too far away.

I'm on a long leash attached to the doghouse. It looks like a clothesline to me. So although I can get out of the doghouse, I can't exactly *go* anywhere. When the milkman comes I ask him to let me loose.

"Excuse me," I say very politely. "Would you mind undoing me? I don't think they meant to leave me tied up, and they've gone somewhere in the car. I think they'd be very grateful if you did, because it's not very nice leaving me tied to a doghouse. I'm not going to run away, because when you leave you'll be shutting the gate. I'm supposed to be guarding the house. It's difficult to do it properly from here. I need to patrol around it a bit."

"Stop that crazy barking!" the milkman says as he leaves the bottles on the doorstep.

I have to watch the sparrows peck holes in the tops and drink the milk and I can't do anything about it.

What rotten luck to have been the only girl in the litter. I bet the others have really nice homes. I bet none of them sleep in a *doghouse*. Anyway, doghouses are so *old-fashioned* for a dog these days, unless you're a real working dog. I wish I were a working dog. Then at least I'd have something to do.

My ears prick up suddenly, all on their own. There is someone at the door of the house! Maybe someone is going to play with me! I run out of the doghouse like I'm fired out of a cannon, only to be choked by my collar when I reach the end of the cord. My legs sort of disappear from under me and I roll over and over. I get up quickly and shake myself. I don't want to look stupid. It wasn't for me, anyway. It was someone collecting for charity. I'm tempted to do it again so that it looks as if I did it on purpose, but there's no one there to see now, so I go back into the doghouse. I feel embarrassed. It looked as if I hadn't figured out the four-legs thing when in fact I was the first in our litter to go from crawling to standing up. Of course the others soon followed. None of my brothers wanted to be outdone by a *girl*. It was my idea to bring the slipper back too, although they chewed it more than I did. So I moved on to chair legs, which weren't as much fun but a real *challenge*.

I'm so bored now I wouldn't even mind if Cyril's mom came out to do her training session with me. She has taken it upon herself to teach me how to *sit, stay,* and *leave it!* Well, it's perfectly obvious to me what *sit* means. She doesn't have to say it slowly, in a loud voice, as if I come from a foreign country. And I hate the way she wags her finger at me. Sometimes, just to be awkward, I pretend I don't know what she's talking about.

"No, Misty! I said *sit,* not lie down."

I also like eating the treat when she is holding it out in her hand asking me to *leave it*. Why would I want to do that? Particularly when it looks as if she's giving it to me.

But the most fun I had was when she first put the leash on me and expected me to walk along at her side. She clearly doesn't understand that us dogs need to sniff at everything as we are walking along. So I'd lie down and make her drag me along the pavement or, even better, go *backward*. Still, even the most fun things get boring after a while, so now I just trot along at the end of the leash, grateful that I'm out of the doghouse.

This time when I'm out of the doghouse, Cyril and I are at the bench again, he on his phone, me waiting for *someone* to throw a ball. I have my head on my paws and now I'm watching some ants busying themselves on the grass in front of my nose. They are moving a bit of candy, and they are so organized. Part of a team. I miss being part of a team. If Ms. Roberts, our gym teacher at school, could see the way I run *now*, I'd be made captain of the soccer team.

I keep on watching the ants. There's nothing for *me* to organize anymore, and I wish there were. Other than move my bone around the doghouse, there's nothing to do. I used to have a planner called a Personal Organizer and it had all sorts of stuff in it. I kept ticket stubs from movies I'd liked, receipts for hot chocolate in the coffee shop, and the ticket for the bus I was on once with Owen

Taylor. But not now. Now there is nothing for me to file away, though I'm sure if I could get my hands on a few sheep, I could organize *them*.

Yes, there's a whole world down in that grass.

I see a group of boys swaggering toward us. I stand up to make myself look bigger. There's something about them I don't like.

One of them stops.

"What you up to, dude?" he says to Cyril. "Should you be out without your mommy?"

Cyril tries to hide his phone and shrinks back into the bench. I can feel the hairs bristle up on the back of my neck. This must be making me look at least twice my size by now. I feel big, anyway. It fills me with confidence. I don't think I'm scared; I just don't like them. I don't have to sniff them—I can already smell them and they smell of meanness and cowardice and boredom.

"Or is that your mommy?" the boy says, pointing at me and laughing.

Now, I can take a joke at the best of times, but this isn't even *funny*. I feel sorry for Cyril. I was bullied at school by Jessica Warner. She and her gang of friends would poke fun at me and spread stupid rumors that weren't true. I growl at the boys. It's the first time I've tried growling properly, and it makes me want to cough.

It's good not being afraid. If I were Cyril, I probably would be. But I'm here to protect him. After all, that is the deal. I give Cyril and his family devotion and loyalty, and they feed me, walk me, and love me back. Well, that is how it is supposed to work.

"I don't think you'll be needing that phone anymore," one of them says, and steps toward us to take it. I growl again, louder. It's a strange, angry, *how dare you?* sort of noise that scrapes the back of my throat.

The boys back off, and I add a snarl and bare my teeth for show. It is very effective.

An old man, who was sitting on another bench a little farther along, gets up and walks toward us.

"You all right, son?" he asks Cyril.

Son? I think. This man doesn't look like Cyril's dad, unless Cyril's dad has gone out in disguise. For a start, he is much older and has shabby clothes on. Cyril's dad would not be seen dead without his suit on and one of his awful novelty ties.

No. This man is definitely not Cyril's dad.

"Get out of here!" he says to the group of boys.

"All right, old man. Keep your hair on!" one of them shouts, and they pull their hoodies over their eyes, dig their hands deep into their pockets, and stroll off, laughing. We all watch them go. I notice Cyril has sweat patches under his arms. I want to feel good about him, lick him to say it's OK, but I can't help thinking that if he'd taken me for a real walk none of this would have happened.

"That's a fine-looking dog," the old man says, ruffling my ears. I like that. Having my ears ruffled. I roll onto my back. I also like having my tummy tickled.

Well, S-O-R-R-Y. But I do. It's a *dog* thing.

"What's her name?"

Cyril remains silent. He's probably still in shock, and I'm pretty sure that his mother has told him not to speak to strangers.

"Well, go on, Cyril, tell him my name!" I say.

"Misty," Cyril mutters, looking over his shoulder in case his mother can see him.

"Mr. T? That's a funny name for a female."

"*Misty*. The dog's name is Misty."

"Ah," replies the old man.

He rests himself on the bench and we all sit in silence for a while. Then Cyril gets up and starts to drag me home. I don't want to go. I like this man. His face is weather-beaten and wrinkled, and he has the bluest eyes. Besides, I think it's rude to go when he has just helped us out. Shouldn't we be inviting him back for a cup of tea?

"Thank you!" I say to him as Cyril yanks me away. "For getting rid of those boys."

It's the next day, and we are back in the park. Cyril is looking anxiously around in case the boys are there again. Then he does something he has never done before. He ties me to the park bench and goes away! I sit there waiting for him to return. After all, I am a dog and loyalty is in my bones.

I check out the area. There is something lying on a bench farther down the path. It is like a huge bundle of clothes. It moves a bit, stretches, and sits up. It is the old man we met the day before! He has a few bags, which he collects together, and then he slowly stands up, puts his hand on his back, and rubs it.

When he sees me he walks toward me, and I wag my tail like mad. I like this man. My tail feels as if it is attached to a motor. It goes around and around, and I couldn't stop it if I wanted to.

"Hello, girl," he says, rubbing my head like he did before. "Has that boy left you here?"

He sits down on my bench.

"It's a fine day, isn't it? Why aren't you out on a nice long walk, eh?" He chuckles. "It's a grand world out there; you don't want to be spending your time tied to a bench."

I totally agree with him. I want to tell him about my circumstances, but just a funny little whimper comes out and takes me by surprise.

"I used to know a dog like you. He was a spirit dog. Dogs with two-colored eyes are believed to be spirit dogs. They guide people. Don't go near a farm, mind you. Farmers hate spirit dogs. You'll freak the animals out. It's your eyes, see. No, you won't be popular if you go to a farm. I bet you're a good companion, though." He goes on. "That boy shouldn't just leave you tied to a bench. It's not right. I'd take you with me if I could, old girl. But I don't want no trouble for stealing a dog. And it would be a hard life for you. I bet you've got a nice warm bed on some sofa somewhere."

"No, I haven't! I live in a *doghouse*! I'd love life on the road. I went on a hiking trip with Mom once and it was great!'

He nods sympathetically.

When he sees Cyril returning, the old man stops stroking my ears. He picks up his bags and shuffles off. He moves slowly, as if his feet cause him pain. I watch him as he goes down the path, his words jumping excitedly in my mind. A *spirit dog*. I like the sound of that.

And this is when I hatch the Plan.

Chapter 3

I spend most of my time lying in my doghouse thinking about the Plan. Sometimes I'll think about the Plan with my eyes shut and sometimes I'll think about the Plan with my eyes open. But all the time I am thinking, planning, and plotting. And sometimes I'm worrying about Mom and Dad. I hope Dad hasn't lost his hearing in the accident, because he loves music. He loves the Beatles, but he loves one type of music in particular: modern jazz.

When I was little he taught me the names of his favorite jazz musicians. I didn't know who any of them were, they were just names, but I remembered them for him because it seemed to make him happy.

I know it seems as if dogs sleep a lot. But it's a fact, in my experience, that there is a lot more going on. When dogs are truly asleep, they dream. And when they dream, it is of running through open fields filled with wildflowers, chasing rabbits or deer. You can see their paws twitching sometimes because in their dream, they are running so fast they are almost flying.

But I'm not usually dreaming about that sort of thing. Maybe that sort of dream will come more often later. Mostly, I am dreaming about being home and Mom and Dad.

Once I dreamed I was at my funeral.

I was in a white coffin on an altar and it wasn't in the local church, it was in a huge cathedral with enormous stained-glass windows. It was dark in the cathedral, but the sun was streaming through the colored glass like spotlights and fell onto the coffin. It was like being at a school dance. In this dream I started to dance in the coffin, and the best thing about the dream was that I was dancing with Owen Taylor!

And although I was inside the coffin, I was also sitting in a pew, observing it all.

A small brown creature stepped into the aisle in front of me. At first I thought it was a fox. It had a long tail with a white tip. It trotted up the aisle and jumped into my coffin. And just before it jumped in, it turned and looked at the me who was sitting in the aisle. It wasn't a fox. It was *me*—as a dog.

Anyway, the Plan is simple, but it does need a lot of thought.

The Plan is to escape!

The Plan is to escape and find my dad and be his *spirit dog,* like the old man said. I liked the idea of being a guide dog. Being a guide dog was going to be awesome.

You don't have to be blind to have one. I'd seen people who use wheelchairs with guide dogs. In fact, I'd watched a show on television about them. One particular dog—a Labrador, I think—could do ninety different tasks. *Ninety!* It could do things like take its human's wallet out and give it to the cashier at the store. Fetch keys and other useful things. Go and get help if needed. Take the laundry out of the dryer. Well, *I* could do all those things. And I'd hang the laundry on the line, as well. *And* I'd sort it. And the best thing of all is that I could be back home again with Mom and Dad! Just like it used to be. Well—*almost.* Maybe they've kept my old room just like it was and I can sleep on the bed. I don't think they'd be too strict about that. And I could go and fetch the paper in the morning and sit by Dad all day long and watch those black-and-white movies he so enjoys.

Sometimes when I'm thinking about the Plan my tail will begin to wag all by itself. *Thump, thump* on the floor of my doghouse. I am happy in my thoughts. And this is how I spend my time. Sometimes with my eyes shut. And sometimes with my eyes open.

Of course, it's all very well *making* a Plan. And

it's all very well *thinking* about a Plan. But it's another thing making it happen.

First — I have to escape.

Second — I have to find my way home.

And third, I don't have the faintest idea where I am.

I figure my old home must be somewhere near Cyril's house — say within a radius of fifty miles. I know this because I read about my death in a newspaper. And only *local* newspapers would bother to make such a big thing of it. You know, the pictures and the captions and the reminiscences.

"She was such a lovely girl," said a neighbor. "Always very helpful. Especially with my mail."

Especially with my mail! I only took a package in for her once! Why couldn't she have said something about me being able to ride my bike standing on the crossbar and seat with no hands?

"She was such a lovely girl. So acrobatic. Do you know, she would ride her bike standing on the crossbar and seat with no hands? AND she helped me with my mail."

But even if I have to travel fifty miles, I still have to escape first.

Cyril has begun to make a habit of leaving me tied to the park bench. I suspect his mother has seen him leaving me in the garage. Really I just want someone to play with me. I'm spending too much of my time being tied up.

I keep a lookout for the old man. Sometimes I can see him across the park, looking in the trash can, and sometimes he just appears, as if he's stepped out of thin air. Either way, my tail seems to notice him first, and it wags and wags. It must be funny to be a dog without a tail. I guess you just wiggle your bottom end.

He always comes and talks with me when Cyril's not there. He's told me how he used to have a dog when he was younger and how he misses the company now. But I want him to tell me if he has a family, and why he's sleeping in the park.

One day he's sitting on my bench as if he's waiting for me.

"Don't mind me," he says to Cyril as we go past. "I'll watch the dog for you if you like."

But Cyril hurries on and leaves me at another bench.

"Over here!" I shout as soon as Cyril is gone. "I'm behind the tree!"

The old man picks up his bags and ambles over. I notice that he's short of breath when he sits down.

"Well, old girl. I must be moving on. It's soon going to be too cold for sleeping in parks. I'll miss our little chats. Just wanted to say good-bye to you and wish you a good life."

He fumbles in his pocket and produces half a mint. It has some fluff clinging to it and it is a little squished, but it is delicious and it makes my breath smell like a candy store.

When Cyril comes back he tells me to stop whining and pulls me roughly by the leash.

But I am crying because I won't see the old man again. I watched him leave the park, and when he got to the gate he turned around and gave me a wave. I feel like I've lost my only true friend.

After that, the park doesn't seem the same. I notice the trees are dropping their leaves. Perhaps

31

they are feeling as sad as I am. I lie there and look up at the sky. It looks just like the jigsaw puzzles my aunt gave me for my birthdays that seemed to be nothing but sky, only none of the pieces are missing. I don't know where she got them, but there was always just one piece missing.

"Never mind, Daisy," she'd say. "Don't waste your time looking for the missing piece. Just see the picture as a whole. I expect that missing piece is down behind someone's sofa."

I am lying down under the bench, wondering why people couldn't put their trash in a barrel and wishing that the old man would come back, when I hear a dog barking somewhere in the park.

"Watch out!" he barks. "Danger!"

I get up to have a better view, and sure enough, I see Danger strolling along the path with their hoodies pulled over their eyes and their hands dug deep into their pockets. It is the group of boys. They stop by the dog who was barking. He must be old, because I don't think he's tied to a bench, yet he's not running away. He's standing his ground and keeps barking at them. One of the boys looks as if he's going to run at the dog but instead takes a well-aimed kick. His boot hits the side of the dog, and he rolls over and yelps. Part of me wants to go over and help, and the other part of me feels scared of the boys and what they may do to me. I hear them laughing as the dog limps hurriedly away. I think they're going to follow him and kick him again, but then one of the boys sees me, tied to the bench, and points at me.

They start to walk toward me, pushing and jostling one another as if they are choosing which one will kick *me*. My paws begin to sweat and my heart is pounding in my chest. I'm not hanging around for that.

I try to run, but Cyril has tied some fancy knot he learned at Boy Scouts and the more I pull, the tighter my leash becomes. The boys are so close now I can smell what they've had for breakfast. I pull back on my haunches and flatten my ears tight against my head. The collar suddenly slips off over my nose, and I am away. I don't stop to look behind me. I just run. I have never run so fast. There is no ball to chase, just open park, and as I run the wind catches my ears and they stream out behind me. I have left those boys a long way back. Full of relief, I bark with joy.

"I'm free! I'm free!"

And all the other dogs in the park, all those dogs in their collars and leashes, answer me.

"Good luck!" they bark, and I am through the park gates and out into the world.

I run past Cyril's road, behind the back of the school, and out into open scrubland. I have never run so fast, or so far. Ms. Roberts would have been proud of me. As I run, birds on the ground fly up into the air, and I shout at them just to scare them a bit more. I run through a patch of dandelions and my tail catches their seed heads and they float upward in the breeze. I splash through a small stream and run through some woods. I have never felt so free.

I come to a halt on the outskirts of a suburb, my tongue hanging out and my whole body panting. It is getting dark. I have no idea where I am and I am tired and hungry. I sniff the air. Some rabbits have been nearby, but there's no sign of them now. I'd like to see a rabbit. Not to eat. I'm OK about not eating at the moment, but I would like the company. Any sign of life would do right now. I feel so lonely. The joy of running away and being free has left me. I miss Mom and Dad more than ever.

It's funny how little things can cheer you up, though. I find a bush and clear out a bed from underneath. Around and around I turn. How good it feels not to be inside that doghouse.

I keep on turning until finally I flop down and sleep. And I dream a real dog dream. My legs must have been twitching. I run through the open fields, but there are no wildflowers. And it is *me* who is being chased. First by the group of boys and then by Cyril's mom. She is in the pink dress and she is yelling at me as she speeds across the ground.

"Come back at *once,* Misty! I paid good money for you!" But I keep on running, and when I wake up I am as tired as when I went to sleep.

It is probably about six in the morning. I guess this because I can hear the song of the birds. I yawn and stretch. I am thirsty as well as hungry. I wander out onto a patch of grass and lick the dew off it. I prick my ears. I can hear the rumble of a garbage truck and the occasional van thundering along a road somewhere. I have to say, my hearing is fantastic now. There will be signs on that road, I think. Perhaps I'll recognize some of the names.

I trot off toward a small row of shops. There is no one in sight and I have a good dig through the barrels that have been left out for collection.

Urgh, this is *disgusting*!

Imagine being reduced to this. Looking for people's leftovers. I find some fries in a bag and a slice of stale bread. They don't smell too bad, so I wolf them down. In the next barrel there is half a McDonald's hamburger. Mom never let me eat junk food. It tastes good. What have I been missing all this time? I'm going to make a habit of going through garbage cans in the future.

The sound of traffic is getting louder now and there seem to be some signs of life. The newsstand opens its doors and a boy on a bike wheels up to collect his newspapers. I'm surprised how pleased

I am to see him and I wag my tail. When he sees me, however, he pushes his bike toward me.

"Scram!" he says. "Go away! Leave me alone!"

I remember that a lot of dogs like to frighten newspaper boys and mail carriers and for a moment—only a moment—I can see the temptation to grab the bottom of his pants and give them a little tug.

"It's OK," I say. "Why would I hurt you? I'm just a little hungry. You don't have a mint or something by any chance, do you?"

"What's all that barking?" A man in an apron comes out of the shop and hands the boy a big bag of newspapers.

"Get!" he says to me. "Dumb dogs! Always going through the trash and getting it in the street.'

"Actually, I haven't done that," I say. "Sorry, though. Have *you* got a spare mint or anything? Not bubblegum, though, because it makes my jaws stick."

"*Go*, I said! Stop that barking."

And the man picks up an old Coke can lying on the sidewalk and throws it at me. I manage to dodge out of the way and run off, my tail between my legs. I try to move with purpose, as if I know perfectly well where I'm going. I don't, but you can't afford to dawdle if you're a dog on your own.

When I'm out of sight I slow down. There is a strong smell of cat. I can feel my heartbeat quicken. I see it, farther along the road. It is a long-haired tabby and it is sitting, lazily washing its paws. I like cats. I like their independence. I like the feeling when they choose your lap, above all other laps, to sit on. Yes, I like cats. Normally. But this cat reminds me of Jessica Warner and how she would preen in front of the mirror in the school bathroom. I hated Jessica Warner. She wore her uniform skirt rolled at the waist so it ended six inches above her knee because it looked cooler that way. And she was always flicking her hair from side to side.

I watch the cat get up and make eye contact. Then, before I can stop myself, I have this incredible urge to chase it down the street.

"I've got you, Jessica Warner!" I shout as I take off after her. "I bet that's wiped that silly grin off your face!"

The cat runs across the road and I run after it. Too late I hear a whirring noise and a loud *clunk*. Then the sound of bottles smashing on the road. I didn't see the milk truck. I dodge a parked car and continue after the cat, which by now has run straight up a tree. It sits there, hissing at me.

"I've never liked you, Jessica Warner! You're mean, spreading those rumors about me. You shouldn't have said those things to Owen Taylor. I don't have a life-size cardboard cutout of him in my bedroom. I hardly even *like* him, and now he thinks I'm some sort of freak. And you look totally stupid with your skirt rolled up. Hasn't anyone ever told you to tuck the label in?"

The cat turns tail and climbs higher up the tree.

"Ha! You'll be stuck up there until someone calls the fire department," I shout.

I stand under the tree and continue shouting at her until a man comes out of a nearby house and throws a bucket of water over me. It's so mean I wouldn't be surprised if he is Jessica Warner's dad.

"Stop that barking!" he shouts.

But I don't care. I shake myself violently, sending an arc of water into the air, which catches the morning sun and makes rainbow patterns all along the sidewalk. Then I get moving.

I can hear the traffic louder now, but I still can't find it. All the roads look the same around here and most of them seem to be cul-de-sacs. Out of desperation I take what I think will be a shortcut through someone's yard. As soon as I round the shed all hell breaks loose.

"Get out! Get out! This is *my* yard," shouts a dog when he sees me. He is *huge*. He must be four times my size and has the most enormous fangs.

I'm backing off now.

"Look, I'm sorry, OK? I took a wrong turn."

He takes a giant leap at me. His neck and his jaws are absolutely massive, and there's clearly no reasoning with him. He's backed me up against the barrels and I've got nowhere to run. He lands inches away from my nose, saliva dripping from his teeth. I don't know why he's not tearing me to pieces until I see that he is attached to a chain.

I see a hole in the broken-down brick wall at the end of the yard. I dodge the heap of scrap metal and dash through the stinging nettles. I'm through the hole now and I look around. I'm in someone else's yard.

Compared to the yard I've just been in, this one is like an oasis. I stand still and listen. I am listening for the sound of another dog. There are other dogs barking now in the neighborhood, but this house doesn't seem to have one. What it does have are guinea pigs in a hutch!

I love guinea pigs. I always wanted some when I lived at home, but Mom would never let me have them.

"I'll end up having to take care of them, Daisy, and I've got enough work as it is."

I wasn't convinced by this. Mom wore a locket around her neck and she always fiddled with it when she was anxious or unsure. I didn't think she was totally convinced about not wanting me to have guinea pigs because she was playing with her locket when she said it.

I go over and have a look at them. There is an orange one and a tortoiseshell one, and they are wrinkling their little noses at me, which makes their whiskers twitch, and making adorable little snuffling noises. I lie down to get on their level. I love guinea pigs, but not so much that I wouldn't *eat* one. I'm absolutely starving, and apart from looking fun to play with, they look pretty *delicious*.

They scuttle back into their hutch. I can't reach them because they have a run made of chicken wire and it has a lid on it.

"Hey! Come back. I only want to *talk*," I tell them.

The dog from the other yard must have woken up the people who live here, because they are very quick to get to the window.

"Hey!" a woman shouts. "Leave them alone! Shoo!" She turns away slightly to talk to someone else in the room. "Darling, there's a fox in the yard trying to eat your guinea pigs!"

A *fox*? This woman clearly needs glasses, but I'm not staying to tell her that. I run around the side of the house and back into the cul-de-sac, practically knocking over the boy with the newspapers, who was just getting off his bike.

"Sorry!" I say as I take off up the street.

After a few more wrong turns I hit a highway. By now it is full of trucks and cars. There are complicated signs telling you things you must not do. No stopping. No passing. No driving over 65 mph. I search for an exit sign. There it is. Just after the sign telling you to buckle up. Greenville. Next exit. I knew it!

We spent a weekend at school doing orienteering and I was in charge of the map. I knew just how to follow the roads. I got an A for leading my team from Main Street in Greenville back to the playground by way of the bus station.

The only trouble is—how to cross to the other side? Most of the vehicles don't seem to be obeying the sign telling them to travel no faster than 65 mph. I wait by the side of the road for a gap in the traffic and shout at them.

"Slow down! Can't you read? No faster than 65 mph! Are you blind or what? I'm trying to cross the road here!"

There is no point in looking left and right until it is safe. I would have looked like one of those bobbleheads people have in the back of their cars. As it is I am beginning to feel dizzy. So I just make a run for it. I run into the road, dodging cars left and right. I can hear the squeal of brakes. The sound of horns being blasted. I think I even hear the noise of bumper hitting bumper. But I just keep running and I am across, under the guardrail and into the fields on the other side. I am running toward Greenville and Mom and Dad. Running toward my cool bedroom with the bed that was a mattress on the floor and the SAVE THE PLANET posters and the pink mosquito net and the window overlooking the backyard.

I keep running for the rest of the day, across fields and through woods. I keep off the roads and, apart from some people on horses in the distance, I don't come across anyone. When night draws in, I make myself another bed in some long grass at the edge of a field and sleep a dreamless sleep.

I wake up to a bright light. At first I think it's morning. Then I see the light is coming from a truck, which is moving across the field toward me. It has three or four headlights attached to the roof as well as the ones in the front, and it lights up the whole field. I can hear the murmur of men talking. I shrink back into the undergrowth. The light picks up a couple of dogs sniffing the ground. They are huge and have an awful lot of face on them. I wonder what they are doing out here. I feel sure that whatever it is, it's against the law. And I don't intend to hang around and find out.

I turn to sneak away, but the white tip of my tail is caught in the beam.

"Fox!" cries one of the men. "Sic 'em, boys."

What's with this fox stuff? I think. Can't they see I'm just a *dog*?

The dogs quicken their pace, barking from deep down inside their bellies. If I weren't so scared I'd be impressed by the noise they are making. I think my own bark hasn't really broken yet. It sounds a bit small and high-pitched. But I am terrified. Imagine being set upon by my own kind. Shouldn't us dogs stick together?

The headlights show only open fields with nowhere to hide, but I take off, the hounds close on my heels and the trundling truck not far behind. This is worse than that dream of being chased by Cyril's mom. I'm fast, but I think those other dogs probably have stamina. Something Ms. Roberts always told me I didn't have.

I look around for a hole I can get into. Surely a real fox must have made a den somewhere? Or a badger? I'm not fussy. But there is nothing. In spite of the fact that I have been running all the previous day, my legs just keep going. I don't even have to think about it. They just keep working while my head is busy thinking of something to do that will throw them off my track.

Suddenly, something rears up in front of me. I stop for a moment, wondering what it is. We both stare at each other in horror and disbelief. It is a young deer. She seems frozen to the spot, and it looks as if her big brown eyes are going to fill up with tears. She looks past my shoulder, sees the other dogs, and she's off. Jumping and bounding across the field in the opposite direction. I start to run the other way, and the bloodhounds quickly change scents. With more barking, they take off after her.

The men in the truck lose interest in me too when they see the deer. I think this is what they've been after all along. But I don't stop running till I get to the outskirts of a wood. Then I flop down, my tongue hanging out and my whole body panting.

I hope she gets away, that poor deer. I can't bear to think of her being torn to pieces by those huge dogs. I don't think she was expecting death when she lay down to sleep in that patch of field. I know, because I wasn't either, and if that deer hadn't been there it would have been me.

It is late afternoon and I turn the corner onto Alexander Avenue. How many times have I come around that corner, swinging my bag after school or pedaling my bike or running breathless because I'm late for dinner? I can't see our house because there is a huge truck parked out front. I stop to get my breath and lick my paw. I cut my pad on some stones as I went across the field and now that I've stopped running it begins to hurt.

I limp along the sidewalk toward number twelve. There are two men carrying something out of the truck into our house. Mom and Dad must have bought a new sofa. Though I don't think much of the color. Maybe they've lost their sense of style since my death. Never mind, it looks comfy enough, and I'll enjoy curling up on those big soft cushions. But there is more. There are chairs and tables and toys! Heavens—they aren't having another baby, are they? To replace *me*? How could they? Surely they are a bit *old* to have more kids?

It is then that I see the sign. It is a big square sign stuck on a post in the yard. It says SOLD.

I sit on the sidewalk and stare at the letters. However hard I try to rearrange them in my mind to say something different—like a message to me—I can't. They're gone. Mom and Dad are gone and haven't left a single clue for me. No note. No phone number.

I watch a woman coming out of the house and walk toward the truck.

"Yes—that box is for the living room. I've put colored stickers on each box so you can tell. Yellow—living room; green is kitchen."

She sees me and stops.

"Hello!" she says, bending down. "Are you friendly?"

I lower my head and wag my tail.

"I used to live here," I tell her. "With Mom and Dad. But now they're gone. Have they left you a note for me or a forwarding address, by any chance?"

She strokes my head.

"You've got no collar on. I wonder who you belong to."

"Mom and Dad," I say.

She stops stroking me and goes into the house. I think she's coming back with a piece of paper with their new address on it, but instead she has one of those bone-shaped biscuits in her hand.

"You poor thing. It doesn't look as if anyone looks after you."

At that moment a small girl comes out of our house.

"Mom—are we getting a new dog?"

The woman shakes her head.

"'Fraid not, darling. Moss wouldn't like it, would he? Two dogs are one too many in this house. Now run up and find your bedroom. It's the one with the window looking over the backyard."

"That's my bedroom," I say after I've eaten the biscuit. Mom always warned me about talking with my mouth full. "Is there still a mattress on the floor and a pink mosquito net?"

But somehow I know there won't be.

"Now, you'd better move on, before Moss sees you. He's a very jealous dog," the woman says, and she goes to talk to the movers. Then she goes back into the house and shuts the door.

I lie down with my head on my paws. I want to cry but I can't. I see a lifetime stretch out in front of me, scavenging in trash barrels. What is going to happen to me? As hard as I try, there is nobody who understands me. Nobody who can comfort me and tell me it'll be all right.

All my hopes and disappointments and realizations of what I now am get stuck in the back of my throat.

Out comes an extraordinary noise. I lie on the sidewalk and howl.

Chapter 4

It begins to get dark. The woman in my old house draws the curtains. Hundreds and thousands of stars are twinkling in the galaxy. I try to see Orion's Belt. And it is there. Three bright stars in a row and then, surrounding the belt, four more bright stars that are supposed to be Orion's body. Orion was a hunter in Greek mythology. I wish now I'd concentrated more in class. When Mr. Pearce was talking about constellations, Jake Harris was distracting me with his ruler.

And then I see another star. It is the brightest star in the night sky. It is my star. Sirius. The Dog

Star. Somehow, looking up at that bright light, I feel comforted. I imagine it is someone watching over me. And it fills me with hope.

The movers have left. The lights in the house are turned off, and I know it is time to move on. But now I don't know where to go. I decide to go down to the train station. It is a place I was never allowed to go alone. It was considered unsuitable and dangerous. But I am free now. I don't belong to anyone, so I can do what I like. Besides, I'm curious. I want to know what it is about a place that makes it *unsuitable*.

A small van is parked at the back of the parking lot, and someone is dishing out soup and bread rolls. There is a shuffling line of people. They don't *look* dangerous. Just tired and hungry. Like me. I think I might have a chance of getting a roll. I am starving again. That little bone-shaped biscuit, although nice, has not filled me up.

I creep slowly toward the van. Before I ran away from Cyril I never crept anywhere. I would trot—my head held high, my tail up. Now my head is down and my tail clamped firmly between my legs. There is a warm smell coming from the van. It smells a bit like Mom's carrot and coriander soup. I lick my lips.

"I recognize you!" says a voice. "You're that spirit dog."

A rough hand strokes the top of my head and I look up. It is the old man from the park.

"What's happened to you?"

I'm so pleased to see him I forget my manners and jump up.

"I ran away. It was after what you said about spirit dogs and such, and I thought I'd try to find Mom and Dad and be their guide dog. My dad's paralyzed, you know. I'm actually a girl. Daisy Fellows."

"People can be very careless with their animals, can't they? But old Jack'll make sure you're all right. You look cold and hungry. Come and sit with us."

Well, yes, I think. It would be nice to go and sit with him, but it's food and water I'm after. It's all very well being patted, but my stomach's rumbling and I'm going to dry up like a prune unless I get a drink.

The old man shuffles over to some sleeping bags piled up in a disused doorway.

"Pip! Wake up! We've got a visitor!"

The tousled head of a boy, a little older than me, appears from the pile of sleeping bags. He has dark hair and a mouth that looks as if he is always smiling. He rubs his eyes, yawns, and stretches.

"What time is it? Is it morning?"

I like the look of him and go over and put my nose by him. You can tell most things you want to know about someone when you give them a sniff. He smells warm and kind and funny and sad. I don't know why people bother with all that handshaking and small talk. Why don't they just give each other a good sniff?

"Where'd you find him?" The boy sits up.

"Looking for something to eat by the soup wagon."

"He must be hungry. He can have my roll, and I've still got an apple core in my bag." Pip rummages in his bag and gives me the piece of apple. Then he does the best thing in the world. He takes a small plastic bowl and a bottle of water out of his bag and offers me a drink.

"Hey! Have you seen his eyes? They're different colors," he says, watching me drink. "He's a lovely boy, aren't you?"

"I'm not a boy, actually," I tell him in between laps of the water. "I'm a girl."

"She's not a boy. She's a girl," the old man says. "I remember her from when I was sleeping in some park or other. She had some sort of name that made me think of the weather. But I can't for the life of me remember what it was."

Oh, please don't remember, I think. I really don't want to be stuck with Misty for the rest of my life.

"Does she belong to anyone?" Pip asks.

"Not by the looks of it. Not anymore. She's got no collar. No name tag. She can be yours now, Pip. Everyone needs a companion sometimes. Especially *you*, right now."

The boy, Pip, ruffles my ears just how I like it,

and I creep nearer his side. He has very brown eyes. But I feel torn. I feel a loyalty to Jack. After all, he was kind to me in the park, and gave me the idea about escaping, and now *he's* giving me his roll to eat as well.

I go back to Jack's side.

"I think you should look after Pip, old girl. He's new to the streets and I'm an old hand at it. Go on, Pip—give her a name."

"Now, let me think. Weather . . ."

Pip thinks for a while and then he begins to smile, and it lights up his face like the morning sun.

"Ray! I'm going to call her Ray!"

I spend my first night as the dog, Ray, as close to Pip as I can get. I don't think anyone sleeps much. It is noisy. There is some shouting and some arguing.

"Don't take any notice of that, old girl," says Jack, rolling up his trouser leg. "They're always at each other. They drink so much they usually can't remember what they're arguing about. It always starts with the same thing, though. Who owns the sleeping bag?"

But I'm not listening. Jack has wrapped newspaper all over his legs and tied them up with string. And some of the paper looks really old.

"You looking at my newspapers, girl? They keep Jack warm, see. It can turn nippy at night and these newspapers do the trick. Remember that, Pip." He turns to the boy. "Remember that, if you're still on the streets when it gets really cold."

Still on the streets? No bed? Apart from those nights under the bushes, I've always had somewhere to sleep. And I wasn't happy under those bushes. And I'm not sure I am going to be happy in the station parking lot either. But at least I have Pip. Jack has asked me to be Pip's dog and so I will. I'll be the best dog anyone's ever had. I will be loyal, obedient, and protect him as best I can.

I want to ask Pip what he is doing in the station parking lot. Why he doesn't have a home to go to and where his mom and dad are. But I don't want to be a nuisance when we have just met. So I lie still, one eye half open, just to make sure that Pip is going to be OK. It seems like a very long night.

* * *

In the morning, Pip tells me we will go and look for food.

"You coming, Jack?" he says to the old man. But Jack shakes his head.

"Not feeling too good today, Pip. It's my chest. Damp socks, you know. You go. Take care. Don't let them take that dog. And don't let them take you either."

Pip grins, puts a knitted hat on, and gives me a little tug. He has made me a collar and leash out of some twine, and I trot happily along at his side. It's quiet in the lot now, and the soup wagon is gone. I can hear Jack coughing as we leave through the gate.

It is still quite early and very few people are around. Out in the street, Pip goes through the trash barrels, just like I did.

"Here we are, Ray. Here's some leftover chicken."

I gratefully chew around the bone. I am impressed that he has fed me before himself.

"Thanks," I say, and wag my tail at him.

"Barbecued chicken's my favorite after spaghetti and meatballs and Thai green curry."

Pip finds a discarded sandwich, a brown banana, and a half-empty can of Coke. He thirstily drinks from the can — only to spit it out seconds later.

"Aargh! Someone put a cigarette out in it. That's disgusting."

I sympathize with him and continue to nibble on the chicken.

We move into the park and Pip goes to sit on the swings.

"You know, Ray," he says, "we've got to be careful. I ran away from foster parents, and if I'm found they'll get me back or lock me up somewhere so's that I don't escape again."

"Me too!" I tell him, and he strokes the top of my head.

"My mom died, see. So I was taken into state care. But it hasn't worked out and . . ." He bends down to whisper in my ear. "I'll let you in on a little secret."

I hold my breath. No one has told me a secret

since Susan Maitland confided in me that her mom had won the lottery and was scared that people would ask her for money if they found out.

"I'm going to look for my dad! He doesn't know, and I've never met him. I'm not sure he even knows he *is* a dad. Mom met him at college when they were seniors, and she moved away before she found out she was pregnant. She told me that she was so happy with me she couldn't see the point in trying to find him and tell him."

I wag my tail and jump up at him, thrilled with the similarity of our stories. Well, of course he hasn't died or become a dog. But we are both looking for our dads and neither of them know of our existence.

"My mom's dead," he goes on, "and she didn't tell me about my dad until just before she died. But she gave me a picture of him." Pip digs into his pocket and produces an old black-and-white photograph of a young man who looks just like him. He shows it to me proudly.

"He looks nice," I say encouragingly.

Other people begin to arrive at the playground,

and Pip decides we should move on. We walk back into town and Pip shows me the library.

"I like it in here," Pip says as we walk up the steps. "I go and read the newspapers and look through the telephone directories for my dad. I haven't found him yet."

"You can't come in with that dog, young man," says a voice behind the desk. "Didn't you see the sign? Guide dogs only."

"But I *am* a guide dog," I say. "Well, I will be when I find my dad."

"Shhh!" the voice continues. "This is a *library*!"

Pip looks disappointed. I want to say he could go on in and I'll wait outside, but he just says "Sorry!" and takes me out. I think that's nice of him, not leaving me, and I give him a little lick to make up for it. He takes his hat and jacket off, and we sit on the jacket at the bottom of the steps. I sit cheerfully at his side, watching. There's plenty to look at and it's warm, being in the sun. Pip seems quite happy just sitting there. I suppose he is making a Plan, like I did. I hope I'll be included in it, whatever it is.

I lie down and put my head on my paws. I shut my eyes. It is getting busy now and lots of people are walking past us. Suddenly I hear a clunking sound by my head. I get up with a start. Someone has tossed a quarter into Pip's hat.

"That's because of you, Ray!" he says, taking the coin out of the hat. Then he changes his mind and puts it back again. "Let's just stay here for a bit, eh? I feel like we're lucky for each other."

By the end of the morning, there is three dollars and fifty cents in Pip's hat. He buys me a bone from the market and a ham sandwich. It feels good, being with Pip.

When we get back to the parking lot Jack is pleased with his sandwich, though I notice he doesn't eat all of it. He coughs quite a lot and puts the rest in his pocket for later.

Apart from Jack, Pip doesn't seem to have any friends either. What I like about him not having any friends is that he talks to *me*. He tells me he's come to Greenville by train.

"When I ran away I knew they'd send the police or the social worker to find me, so I thought

I'd better get on a train. I just got on the first one that was leaving. It was exciting. I had to jump over the barriers and I only got on the train because someone had gotten their coat caught in the door and it hadn't locked right. I had no idea what direction I was going in. I had to get off at Greenville because I didn't have a ticket and the conductor was coming around. I had to hide in the bathroom until the train stopped at the station. That's how I met Jack, in the parking lot. So I was lucky, wasn't I? I wouldn't have met you either!" He lays his head on my neck.

For the next few days our routine is the same. We find some food somewhere, go to the park, and sit on the library steps. Often the best food is from the farmers' market after the produce people have gone. There are some really good things. Apples, peaches, only a little bruised. I wish Mom knew about waiting for the market to pack up. She always wanted to get there early to get the best.

I'm not giving up on finding Mom and Dad,

even though I'm with Pip now. And if I do, I'll show Mom the market when they've closed down. See, that would all be part of being a guide dog. *Showing* her things. And if I do find Mom and Dad, and Pip doesn't find *his* dad, maybe he can come and live with us.

There's so much I want to know about Pip. Has he ever been to Turkey? Did he have a girlfriend? Where did he go to school? But he hasn't told me these things yet and I can't get him to understand that I want to know.

I try staring at him very hard to project my thoughts into his. Sort of like a psychic. But he just laughs and strokes my neck.

"What *is* it, Ray? Are you hungry?"

Then one day the librarian comes out and asks us to move.

"You're making people not want to come into the library," she says. "Why don't you go home?"

"We don't have a home," I snap at her. "Isn't that *obvious*?"

But Pip just says "Sorry," and we get up and leave.

We walk along the sidewalk. There is a family in front of us with a woman pushing a carriage with a wailing child.

"Jodie!" she shouts. "Where are you?" Someone pushes past us — a girl about my age — and there is something familiar about her. I look at her. She's eating an ice cream and it's dribbling down onto her pretty dress. It's the dress that looks familiar, I realize. It's turquoise with pink flowers on it. Then I realize it's *my* dress she's wearing! It couldn't have been anyone else's because my auntie made it for me and I chose the fabric with her. What is this girl doing in my dress? And then I remember Goodwill and how when my grandfather died, Mom sorted out his clothes and took them there. I remember wondering what she would think if she saw someone wearing her dad's suit or nice Fair Isle sweater that Grandma had knitted for him. And now here was a girl wearing my dress! Mom must have taken *my* things to Goodwill too. How many other girls are walking around in my clothes? I wonder. Who's got my new skinny jeans that I'd only had for a couple of weeks? And my fake Abercrombie and Fitch hoodie I bought in Turkey?

I want to go and say something to her, but Pip is crossing the road and I don't want to lose him. I am wondering now what they buried me in. I hope it wasn't the bridesmaid dress I wore at my cousin's wedding. That was ghastly and made me look completely childish. It had puffy sleeves and a full skirt. They told me I'd be able to wear it as my prom dress if I let the hem down. Honestly, everybody at school would have laughed at me if I'd shown up in that. I'd like to have been buried in my new coat with the fake-fur collar and, under that, the beautiful long sea-green dress with the thin straps I saw when I was out shopping with Mom.

When we get back to the station Jack hasn't moved from his usual spot. His feet are sticking out from underneath his makeshift sleeping bag as if they can't bear to be contained and had to make a break for freedom. I go over and lick his face. He seems hot in spite of the fact that the weather has turned and is getting colder. His clothes are damp too.

"He's not well, Pip," I say. "Can't we get him to the hospital or something?"

Pip kneels down at his side.

"Jack! Are you all right?"

But Jack doesn't stir. His breath is rasping.

"Come on, Ray. We'll have to find a pharmacy and get him something."

I wag my tail. *Good idea,* I think.

We leave Jack where he is and go back into town. We find a supermarket that has a drugstore in it, and Pip leaves me tied up outside.

"You're not allowed in the store, Ray. So you'll have to stay here. If anything happens to me you have to get out of here. If anyone thinks you're with me they may put you in the pound. Maybe go back to the station if you can find it. Do you understand?"

I wag my tail at him again. It seems the best way to show my agreement. But what on earth is going to happen to him, I want to know? As far as I can see he is going to get something that will help Jack get better and we will give it to him and everything will be all right.

"Good luck!" I say. "Take care!" I'm beginning to feel uneasy about the whole thing. Pip goes into the store and I sit down and wait for him.

It is just like having to wait for Mom when *she* went shopping. "I'm just going to run into the shop, Daisy, I won't be two seconds!"

A million, squillion seconds later she'd be hurrying back to the car.

"Sorry, darling—there was such a *line*! And then I couldn't decide whether to buy the brown one or the green one. So I bought both!"

After a while Pip runs back out of the store.

"Quick, Ray," he says, and bends down and unties me. But just as he does, a man and a woman come up behind him. They are wearing uniforms, but I don't think they are the police. For a start, the man has a grubby mark on his jacket where he dropped something he was eating. I am sure that policemen aren't allowed to have grubby marks on their uniforms. They are probably not even allowed to *eat* in their uniforms. I suddenly have an image of a lot of policemen eating their sandwiches in their hats and underpants.

"We have reason to believe that you have taken something that does not belong to you. Without *paying* for it. Would you please empty out your pockets, sir?"

Pip does as he is told and takes out a box of pills from his jacket.

I look at him. I can see for a moment, in his eyes, the temptation to make a run for it. But the man has a firm grip on his arm.

"They're for a friend. He's very sick. I wanted to give them to him," says Pip, with a look at me that says, *Help me out here, Ray.* So I chip in.

"Look. Pip is not a thief. It's just that we haven't got any money and Jack is sick. It's his damp socks, you see. He's got some sort of chest infection and the pills are supposed to make him better. Though personally, I thought we should have taken him to the hospital."

"This your dog?" says the woman. "It hasn't got a collar or tags."

Pip looks at me sadly.

"No!" he says. "I don't know who it belongs to."

"Looks like a customer for the dog pound, then," the man says, taking his phone out of his pocket.

A small crowd of people have gathered around like they're watching a piece of street theater.

I remember what Pip said about getting out of here, and as his eyes widen I know I have to make a run for it. And I do. As I race for the corner, I can see Pip being led back into the store. The small crowd is still there. I want to go back and help him. Perhaps go for the man's throat or bite the woman's calves. I know this is sheer bravado and also that hanging around with a piece of string around my neck is not a good option. So I keep on running. But it isn't the joyous run I first made in the park, when I escaped from Cyril. It is more like the dream. And I run blindly, scattering people as I charge along the pavement. My mouth is dry and my tongue is hanging out and I can feel saliva gathering in the corners of my mouth.

"What's up with that dog?" I hear someone say.

"It's probably got rabies. Did you see its eyes?"

"Rabies!" someone else screams.

Rabies? I think. Oh, how ridiculous! Where was I going to get rabies from?

But by now there is a stream of people chasing me along the sidewalk. My heart is racing even faster than my legs. If only Pip were with me. If only I had wings like that guy in the myth who flew too near the sun. I try to think of his name as I tear across the square. But all I can remember is staring out the window during class and watching Owen Taylor play soccer. I was sure he had winked at me and I took no notice of Mr. Pearce droning on about the dangers of the sun. Then I realized that Owen Taylor had just gotten some mud in his eye.

"He should have been wearing SPF 30, shouldn't he?" said Jessica Warner to a giggling class. "Look. Daisy Fellows is bright red. Maybe *she* got too close to the sun!"

It's because of all this thinking that I don't see the bicycle. It shouldn't be on the sidewalk anyway. It's dangerous riding on the sidewalk and can cause an accident. Which is exactly what happens.

As I race past, my piece of trailing string gets caught up in the pedals. The bike and the man riding it topple over and we all go crashing to the ground.

Then I suddenly remember. "Icarus!" I say. "Icarus! Icarus!" I'm sure it must sound as if I'm swearing bloody murder as I fall.

Another crowd of people gathers around. Perhaps not as many as probably collected by our car when it crashed. But still, quite a sizable crowd. More than were outside the supermarket.

"Is the dog all right?" an elderly woman asks.

"Damn the dog," says the man, crawling out from underneath the bicycle. "Doesn't matter about the dog! What about me? I've hurt my ankle and I've torn my pants!"

"You shouldn't have been riding on the sidewalk, pal!" someone shouts out.

"Yes! That's just what I was thinking," I say. "What do you think the road's for?" I begin to sound like my dad so I shut up.

"Oh, you poor thing," says another person, detangling the string and stroking my head. I look wildly around me to see if the Rabies People are there, but they must have given up a few blocks back.

"Does this dog belong to anyone?" comes a stern voice. A voice of authority. The kind of voice that wears a uniform. And I am right! A policeman walks up to the scene. He *definitely* doesn't have any stains on his uniform, and I can see my face in the shine on his boots as he approaches me. "And what were you doing riding on the sidewalk, sir?"

We all murmur in agreement.

"What do you think the road's for?"

The policeman gets out his walkie-talkie. "OK!" he continues. "So no one owns the dog?"

A few people shake their heads. There is a lot of crackling coming from his handset, and holding my string firmly, he walks to the corner to get better reception.

I know what he is doing. He is calling the dog pound.

Chapter 5

My kennel cell is between Max, a bull terrier, and Toby, a mutt.

Neither of them says much. In fact, neither of them says *anything,* and I only find out their names because one of the wardens is showing two people around.

"This is Max," she says, stopping outside his door. "Max is afraid of strangers and loud noises. He'd prefer a quieter life and could live with children, provided they're not very young. Do you have children?"

The couple look doubtful and then suddenly remember that indeed they do have *two very young children*.

"Now this is Toby," she goes on, ignoring me completely. "Toby is a misunderstood dog who does not do well with stress. He would like to relax in a home where little is expected of him. But he does like doing obstacle courses, like running through tunnels and over jumps."

Golly, what tunnels? I think. Sounds fun — a little like gym class. As long as there's no rope climbing. For some reason I've never been good at climbing ropes.

"Come along, Daisy!" Ms. Roberts would cry. "Think *monkey*!"

Perhaps that's what they'll say when it comes to my turn. "This is Ray. She hasn't been with us long so we don't know much about her, but she's absolutely hopeless at climbing ropes."

"What about this dog with the funny eyes?" the man asks.

"Ah. We can't tell you much about her. She

hasn't been with us very long. She's awaiting assessment."

They nod at me.

"Well, I can tell you all about me if you want," I say, jumping up at the bars to get their attention. "I like playing soccer, riding a bicycle, going to the movies, and baking cakes. I think I would like running through tunnels and over jumps too. I'm not at all worried by strangers—in fact, my mom always said I was good with people."

"She barks too much," the woman says. "It would not be good for the *children*."

I sigh and lie down on my cushion. I look around me.

"How long have you been here?" I ask Max. "Who were you, before you were a dog?"

But Max just stares at me and goes back to his corner. I remember that Max is worried by strangers so I think I'll talk to Toby, but he is chewing on a bone so I decide not to disturb him. Really, where is the *communication*? It strikes me how silent the place is. No one seems to have anything to say. It is as if they've had their personalities sucked out of them.

I am thinking about having your personality sucked out of you and the fact that I went through the wrong door. The woman in the Job Center had twice told me to go through the door on *the right*. And I went through the door on *the left*. Perhaps the door on the left was a prototype and because of all the cutbacks they hadn't been able to afford to put a lock on it. Really! What if you couldn't read? They should at least have put a chain across it.

And now, suddenly, I know why I was supposed to go through the right-hand door. You're not supposed to remember who you've been in a previous life! Max and Toby, well, they must have gone through the door on the right and had their memories erased. I don't want to lose my memories. Getting my left and my right muddled up was an advantage to me this time. If I forgot everything about me I wouldn't be me. I want to still be me.

I sit in the quiet space. Only the sound of the warden's voice drifts over the silence.

"Now, George here loves to eat and to play with his squeaky toy, but cats and small furry animals are a no-no."

The dog pound is situated near a farm in the middle of nowhere. There is a fenced-off area, surrounded by fields, where we are taken to *do our business*. Those fields look so inviting that I long to stretch my legs and run through the grass. I stand by the wire fence and stare into the distance, wondering what has happened to Pip. And when I'm in my kennel cell I sit in my corner and wonder what has happened to Pip. And then the wondering turns to worrying. I imagine him locked in a police cell or back with his foster parents. Although I've just met Pip, I feel very close to him. I think it was the photograph that sealed our friendship.

And when I'm not worrying about Pip I worry about Jack. He is probably dead now, without those pills Pip got. And all because of his damp socks. Mom always went on about damp clothes and not going to bed with wet hair. "You'll get pneumonia!" she'd say.

I never used to worry. Well, I suppose I worried the first day of school that no one would like me, and I worried when it came to exams in case, after they said, "Now turn over your papers," I couldn't answer anything other than what my name was. But I wouldn't say I was the worrying type. As a dog, though! The responsibilities of being a dog are *enormous*. You have to make sure your owner is safe. You have to make sure that no one robs the house when they're out. And that can mean being worried *all day*. At the moment I'm worried that Cyril and his mom might come to the dog pound looking for me, even though I must be miles away from them by now.

My kennel is near the front desk. This means that I know of all the comings and goings at the pound. I can watch the girl who sits at reception eating candy when she thinks no one is looking and using the phone to make personal calls. There is a different girl who sits there sometimes doing her nails.

I have learned that all us dogs have a card with our particulars on it, pinned to a board by the front desk, and our fate is dictated by which way the card is facing. I know this because a nice man in a hat, who was doing volunteer work, was brushing one of the dogs up by the front desk.

"That's Bertie, isn't it?" said the girl at the desk, and she took his card down and turned it around.

"Why are you doing that?" the man asked.

"Bertie's got to go. I meant to turn his card around this morning. No one wants him and he snapped at one of the cleaning people yesterday."

"Where's he going?"

"He's going to be put down."

"Oh, no he's not!" said the man, grabbing the card and tearing it up. "He's coming with me. I'm not letting him be put down. Come on, Bertie! We're going home!"

The girl at the desk and I looked on in amazement as the man opened the door and took Bertie over to his car.

"Well, I never!" I heard the girl say. "Whatever next!"

The words "going to be put down" rolled around my mind for the rest of the day. So that's what happens when a dog gets taken to that little room at the end of the corridor. I had noticed that they never come back. I only hope that it is quick.

The staff refer to the dogs that no one wants as "sticky" dogs. Dogs that stick around. Max and Toby are definitely sticky dogs, and I wonder if either of them takes any notice of the cards and which way they face. I find I am constantly checking on mine now. So far no one has been interested in taking me. I must learn to keep quiet, I suppose. Actually, if I'm honest I haven't wanted anyone to take me, so perhaps I'll go on telling them what's what. Though I wouldn't have minded if the nice man in the hat had come back for me.

But really it's Pip I want to come in through the door and claim me. Though I don't think they'd let Pip take me. They do all sorts of checks and go and visit the homes of the interested owners.

They wouldn't be too impressed with a pile of cardboard and some old sleeping bags. I could tell them different, though. That it's not where you are but who you're with. And that in my opinion, Pip takes better care of me than Cyril and his family ever did. The Animal Control people *would* probably be impressed with a pink furry toilet seat cover. But what do they know? They think dogs are dogs. But I know otherwise.

Max is the first to go.

They give him a biscuit and a pat on the head and lead him off to the little room. I hope with all my might that he believes he is going to a quieter life. And in many ways I suppose he is. I wonder if this is the end of the line for Max. Is he still a soul? Will he be in the Job Center by now? Certainly, unlike me, he seemed to have no recollection of who he'd been in the life before. But presumably when he gets there he'll still remember being Max. Perhaps, with time, even though I went through the wrong door, I'll forget too.

I go over some things to remember in my head. Henry VIII's six wives, for a start. Their names and what happened to them. Divorced, beheaded, died. Divorced, beheaded, survived. I can't remember, though, if Jane Seymour was beheaded or just died, but I don't think that matters. I can still remember our telephone number and the plate number of Dad's car.

It's a few days later and I come back from *doing my business* and find that my kennel has been scrubbed out and I have been put on the other side of Toby, next to a blank wall. Does this mean the end for me? My card is still facing the same way, but I remember Mom telling me that in some hospitals the patients that weren't going to last the night were moved to the end of the ward. They'd done this with Grandad. The day before he died they put him at the end, near the exit door. He had a wall on one side and an empty bed on the other. There was a picture on the wall of a boat battling through the waves. It was probably the last thing he saw before he died. Well, I hope so. You wouldn't want your last view to be someone emptying out a bedpan.

I am thinking about my grandfather and I hear a faint voice at reception.

"We're looking for a dog for my husband. A dog that would be a good companion and could be trained to do simple things."

My ears suddenly prick up.

"What sort of simple things?" asks the girl at the desk.

"Oh, like taking a wallet out of a pocket, for instance." The woman clears her throat.

At first I think they must be pickpockets and that this is a novel idea, getting a dog to do it. But when she speaks again I know who it is. It is Mom! We watched the program about guide dogs together!

Some chatting goes on that I can't hear, probably some form filling, and then, coming into sight, is Mom pushing my dad in a wheelchair. I practically turn a somersault I am so excited. It is like a prayer has been answered. There is Mom, looking a bit thinner and tired, but still Mom. She's cut her hair shorter, but I don't mind. And there is Dad, sitting upright in his chair as she pushes him along the corridor. Since the accident he's grown a beard, and his hair is flecked with gray. He has a look on his face that tells me that this idea of getting a guide dog was definitely not his. I am excited and sad at the same time. Dad will need a lot of looking after, I can see, but I'll be proud to do it.

"This is Ben. He likes splashing in puddles but probably wouldn't be very good at fetching things."

"Mom! Dad!" I cry. "It's me! Daisy! I'm over here! Look in my kennel. I've been trying to find you, but you've moved. I don't mind, really — it would be fun to live in a new house, and you've probably got elevators and hoists and things in it."

"Gosh, that dog makes a lot of noise, doesn't it?" says Mom. She bends down to look at Ben. "*He's* rather sweet. Darling, what about this fellow?"

"No! You can't take *him*! I can do all the things other dogs can do and more." I hesitate for a moment, remembering Jessica Warner and not wanting to show off too much. "Cats and small animals are probably a no-no, but other than that, take me! Take me!" I jump up and down at the railings, managing to tip my water bowl over at the same time.

"I'm sorry about all the noise," says the girl. "This dog hasn't been here very long. I don't know what's got into her. She's normally as quiet as a mouse."

I don't believe in omens, but this morning a bird flew smack into the window. The window was too high to see what happened to it, but it hit with such force that I don't imagine it survived.

I watch Mom push Dad up to my door. She stops and peers at me.

"Oh, *you're* a sweetie," she says, and bends down to get a closer look.

I feel as if my heart is bursting out of my chest and I leap up at the door.

"Yes, Mom — it's your daughter. You can take me home now. I'll be so good. I know I won't have a bedroom to keep clean, but I won't leave any bones lying around and I promise not to chew any slippers and I won't dig holes in the yard and I'll come when you call me and—"

"Look, Dennis. This little dog is so full of energy. Why don't we take *her*? There's something about her I like. I'm sure we can stop all the barking—she must be fed up being cooped up in here. I wonder what her story is?"

"She was probably abandoned *because* of all that barking," my dad says.

My father and I look at each other, and all the color drains out of his face, like he's a bottle that someone has suddenly tipped upside down.

"No! I couldn't live with this dog. Look at its eyes. It would just remind me of Daisy. It's hard enough as it is without thinking of her every time I look at it."

"But, Dad—it *is* me."

In desperation I roll over onto my back, trying to make myself as appealing as possible. Then, when that doesn't seem to work, I get up and try to lick his hand through the bars.

"Dad! Dad! I keep telling you, it's *me*! I'd comfort you. I'd always be around and I wouldn't argue much. You've got to change your mind and take me with you. I'll never complain or judge you or be embarrassed by your jokes."

"Let's go," my father says. "Perhaps a dog isn't a good idea after all."

As Mom turns the wheelchair around I try again.

"Take me. *Please* take me. Don't leave me here. I didn't mean to break those photo frames by your bed. It was an accident. The blanket got caught up when I was jumping on it. I'm really, really sorry. I won't do it again."

"Does that dog ever stop making noise?" I hear Mom say. This is definitely my mother. She was *always* telling me I was making too much noise. "I imagine it would be difficult to find a home for a dog like that," she goes on. "It's a shame, because she looks like such a sweet little thing." She puts her hand to her neck and pulls out her locket, twisting it around her finger.

The girl nods in agreement.

"I can give you the number of the Assistance Dog people if you like."

And I watch them go back down the corridor. Dad's wheelchair makes a funny little noise like some small creature is stuck to the wheel and is making a squeak every time it hits the floor. I can't believe I've seen them and now I can't believe they're gone. I can't believe they've turned around and disappeared, leaving me here. All on my own. How can they not know it's me?

"Please don't go. I'm trapped in this body of fur, your daughter, who you always said you loved. If you leave me here you'll never see me again. I know you don't know it, but I came looking for you and you never left a forwarding address. Why don't you look back? Why don't you see me?"

I strain my ears till I can't hear the squeaking anymore and then I lie down on my cushion and I'm howling again. For my lost childhood and the girl I was and my lovely mom and dad. For the lost opportunity that I know won't happen again. For the grief I know they are going through. I want to tell them it is all right and that I'll always be with them. There are no tears running down my face to comfort me. I just have a huge pain in my chest, as if someone's ripped my heart out and stuffed the hole up with old newspapers.

They've left the building now, and in the distance I can hear their car drive away.

As I said, I don't believe in omens, but the morning of our crash a young blackbird flew out of the porch straight under Mom's foot as she was walking in. It broke its neck.

Later that day I notice that my card has been turned the other way.

Chapter 6

All the dogs are let out at a regular time, and today I am allowed out to the back field with them. The workers always stand around and chat, drink coffee, and smoke cigarettes, while we mind our own business.

I am sitting by the fence, wondering what will happen to me. I'm not afraid. Perhaps I'll get a better job next time around—a *qualified* one. I wonder how far back I'll remember. For instance, if I went out the wrong door again, and if I came back as, say, a human, would I remember being a dog? And would I remember being Daisy as well as being a dog? When I was Daisy I couldn't remember being anyone else. I think about Henry VIII's wives again but am no clearer as to what happened to Jane Seymour. Hey—perhaps I *was* Jane Seymour in a previous life!

I am just imagining being Jane Seymour when I notice a plume of smoke rising from the dog pound.

"Fire!" someone shouts. The workers rush into the building, and I keep thinking about Jane. There is a lot of smoke now, which sets off the fire alarm. Some of the dogs are barking. Through the mayhem I hear a voice.

"Ray!" it says. "Ray! Over here. Quick!"

I look toward where the voice is coming from, and there, right by the fence, is Pip. My heart almost leaps out of my fur.

"Pip!" I shout. "You're all right! How did you get here? How's Jack? What's going on?"

"Shhh, Ray," he says. "Don't make so much noise—they'll hear us."

I see that he has cut a hole in the fence and that he is holding open the wires.

"What about the others?" I ask. "Perhaps they'd like to get out too."

I look back at the other dogs. There is Toby, sniffing around, and George, busy with his squeaky toy. I don't think Toby would be able to cope with the stress, and none of the others seem interested. I squeeze through the wire and give Pip a big lick.

"Let's get out of here before they catch us. I set some newspaper on fire and put it in one of the trash cans to create a diversion."

"What a brilliant idea!" I congratulate him and give him another lick. Then I run around him in small circles, telling him all the things that have happened since we parted outside the supermarket.

"Be *quiet*, Ray, they'll hear us. Oh, no! They did! Let's go!"

I glance behind me and see one of the workers making her way toward the hole in the fence.

"Hey! Come back with that dog!" she shouts. But we start to run. We run through the long meadow grass, scattering wildflower petals as we go. Poppy, corn cockle, oxeye daisy. I know them all thanks to Mom and her love of flowers. It must look like a wedding with all this colored confetti.

We cross one field and into the next. The skylarks are singing for a beautiful day. If Pip had thrown me a stick I would have fetched it. I definitely wouldn't have fetched a stick for Owen Taylor. And as we round the corner we come across some cows.

I'm not sure if they are Guernsey or Holstein. I rack my brain for the right page in the *I Spy Book of Farm Animals*. I think you get twenty points for a black-and-white cow. Whatever their breed is, they are all looking at us and have herded together into quite a tight-knit group.

We stop running. I am standing by Pip. Well, I'm standing *behind* Pip.

I feel all the hairs on the back of my neck stand up in fright. Mom and I were chased by a bull when I was little, and I can still remember flying along at the end of her hand as she raced for the gate. She wore a floral dress, like the meadow we have just run through, and for some reason I had on a woolen hat and leggings. I must have boiled.

Pip stands his ground.

"What shall we do?" I ask.

"Don't bark, Ray. You'll make it worse."

The cows in front lower their heads and start to come toward us. They have pretty big horns.

We begin to back off a bit. I am all for running away, but Pip stands his ground and I love him for it. I love him more than Owen Taylor.

"Shoo!" he says, and waves his arms. "Get away with you!"

They are quite near us when they stop. They seem to be looking at me. I think we all must have been holding our breath. Then they snort in unison, shake their heads, turn, and gallop off. I am surprised and then I remember what Jack said to me when we met in the park. About my eyes freaking out farm animals.

"Come on, Ray, let's run for the other field before they change their minds and come back," says Pip.

We turn to go. At that moment I would have run anywhere with him. But running toward *us* are two of the officers from the dog pound.

"Come back here *at once*! That dog is not your property!"

"*I am!*" I shout back at them. "I belong to Pip. You can't take me back now. Besides, you turned my card around, so you didn't want me anyway."

And with that we run after the cows, leaving the officers far behind. And the faster we run, the more crazy the cows go, until they are bucking and snorting and mud is flying in the air and I am laughing and laughing.

"It's *you*, Ray!" Pip pants. "There's something about you that's driving them nuts! Ha! Ha! You *good* dog!"

I like that. Pip calling me good.

We are laughing so much I don't think either of us sees the Land Rover with the farmer in it. He pulls up and gets out. He is holding a shotgun.

"What do you think you're doing on my land?" he shouts, waving the gun at us. "I've a good mind to shoot that dog. And I'm perfectly within my rights to do it. Not only are you *trespassing* but you've scared my cattle. They're in calf and this stupid behavior will probably make them all miscarry. Do you realize how many hundreds of dollars that will cost me? Why can't you people stick to the trail?"

I'm sure I'm not alone in feeling sick to my stomach.

"I'm sorry, sir," says Pip. "We didn't mean it. We—I mean, I—wasn't thinking straight. I didn't see a sign for a trail."

"Are you calling me a liar? I have to put up a sign for you awful people. Trails? Bah! Troops of city people walking over my property! Trails should be abolished."

The farmer turns back to his Land Rover and goes to take something out. I am sure it is going to be extra bullets. He seems very angry. He produces a piece of paper.

"What's your name?" he says, taking a pencil stub out of his pocket.

"Uh—Phillip. Phillip Seagrove."

"And what's your address, Phillip Seagrove?"

Pip reels off a number and some street.

"I'll be sending the vet's bill to your parents, then. And you've got five minutes to get off my land or I'll call the police. And as everything that you can see is my land, you'd better get going. And *keep away from my cows.*"

The farmer reverses his Land Rover and tears off after the disappearing herd. I sit down on the grass and shake. Mom had a miscarriage when I was eight. I was going to have a baby brother, and Mom and Dad were so excited. They decorated the spare bedroom and bought baby things and talked endlessly about what they would call him. I hated it. And I hated the idea of someone else in the family. I'd have to share my toys with him and later I'd have to babysit for him and I wouldn't have Mom and Dad to myself anymore and wasn't I good enough for them?

And then Mom lost the baby. She had this miscarriage. She went to the hospital and when she came back she cried and cried and they gave all the baby things away and turned the baby's room into a study for Dad. Though he never studied anything. And it was my fault. Because if I hadn't hated the baby so much it wouldn't have died. And now all those cows are going to lose *their* babies and that is all my fault too.

"Come on, Ray. We have to get out of here."

But I won't budge. I feel too depressed. And I think that spirit-dog thing is probably a load of nonsense. I don't think those cows ran away from me because I have different-colored eyes. I think they ran away from me just because I'm a *dog*.

"Ray! Come *on*! We don't want them to take you back to the dog pound, do we?"

I kind of want to shake my head, but the shaking-the-head muscles only seem to work if something is irritating it. Like an insect. Of course I don't want to go back to the dog pound. I want to be with Pip. I'll do anything for him. Anything he asks. Besides, I don't want to stay in the farmer's field. I think he's probably mad and will return with his shotgun loaded.

I struggle to my feet. I have burrs stuck to my fur.

"Is your name really Phillip Seagrove?" I ask.

"Come on, Ray," he says. "We need to get out of here."

We are walking along the street now and it is getting dark. The soup wagon is back in the station parking lot.

"I'm starving, Ray. Bet you are too. Let's get some rolls and go and see Jack."

"Jack?" My ears prick up. I like the way I can get them to change shape. I can make them pointed, floppy, or flat. I can raise one ear independently of the other and I can make them fly when I run into the wind.

"Is Jack all right, then? I've been worried. What about his damp socks?"

And there he is. Sitting on a piece of cardboard, wrapped in a sleeping bag.

"Ah, you're back, Mister Pip, and you've got Ray. Well done, boy! Did that trick with the newspaper I told you about work?"

Pip nods. So it wasn't his idea after all. But I love him, nevertheless. I love the way he grins at me and strokes my head. I love his hair that flops in his eyes and makes him look like a rock star, and I love the fact that he — well — seems to love *me*. Apart from Mom and Dad, I don't think anyone else ever has.

I run over to Jack, wagging my tail, and lick him.

"I'm so happy to see you. I was really worried," I say.

"I expect you thought you wouldn't see me again, didn't you? Well, old Jack got better, thanks to Pip. He told the store manager about me and they took me off to the hospital, gave me a load of pills, and now I'm as right as my left foot. And Pip just got a telling off."

In the morning, Pip leaves me with Jack.

"I'm going into town, Ray. I don't want anything to happen to you again, so you stay here. Jack'll make sure you're all right."

He hasn't left me before, and I am anxious. Why can't I be with him? Has he stopped liking me?

I sit down next to Jack and watch Pip disappear across the lot.

"Don't worry, old girl," says Jack, "he'll be back. He's just gone to get something for you."

Is it my birthday? What is the date today? Actually, when *was* my birthday?

I can't quite remember. I'm not trying to remember my birthday as a *dog*—because that would have been when we had the car crash and that was . . . Well, when was *that*? Was it Christmastime? Perhaps Dad and I were going to the supermarket to buy a turkey. I can't quite remember. No, it is my birthday as Daisy I am trying to remember. It sort of swims in and out of my memory like a goldfish.

I am still trying to remember my birthday when Pip comes back. He is carrying a small brown paper bag and is looking very pleased with himself.

"Here we are, Ray. You're official now. They won't take you away from me again." And out of the bag he takes a bright-blue collar and on the collar is a tag. And engraved on the tag in big letters is the word RAY. This certainly *feels* like my birthday, whether it is or not.

"Thank you, Pip. I feel really special now,"
I say.

But what is even better than *my* name is that
on the back of the tag it says:

PIP.

Ray and Pip. I wear it like a locket around my
neck. Ray and Pip. And it nestles on my fur close
to my heart.

I want to know when we're going to look
for Pip's dad. I think we've been in the station
parking lot for too long. Besides, I can't remember
the license number of Dad's car anymore and it
bothers me. I'm sure he had a blue car, but when
I try to think of the plate number it all goes fuzzy.
I think I need some fresh air. Henry VIII's wives
have completely escaped me now. This worries
me. What will happen if I stop remembering who
I really am?

It seems that Pip is trying to get some money to
buy a train ticket. He has an idea that his father
might be living in the same town where he and
his mom went to college.

"We're going to find him, Ray! Even if I have to call every number in the phone book!"

He's left me with Jack a few times to see if he can get any jobs. He's already swept an old lady's driveway, washed a car, and carried stuff to the dump. He's even been paid for walking some dogs! He found an old dog leash at the dump. He showed it to me.

"You'll have to wear this sometimes, Ray, when we go traveling."

I looked at him. I hoped he could see my mouth turning down with disapproval.

Pip is coming toward me now across the station parking lot.

"I've got enough, Jack!" he says. "We'll go tomorrow!"

And Jack nods and puts his hand on my back.

"It's time now, that's for sure. It'll be good for your soul to move on. I hope you find your dad. Don't forget to send old Jack a postcard!"

But we all know that Jack would never get it without an address.

"I'll miss you, Jack," I tell him. "If it weren't for you I'd still be with Cyril and I'd never have tasted freedom. You've shown me what's possible in a dog's life."

I nuzzle up to him. He smells of old books and newspapers and the ocean. We sleep.

I dream Jack is on a large wooden sailing ship with acres of sails. He is at the helm and a huge wave hits the boat side on. Hundreds of silver fish are left flapping on the decks, and as the boat goes up and down the fish slide from side to side. I watch the ship sail away and as it goes over the horizon there is a green flash and Jack and the boat are gone.

We buy a ticket and get on the train. I'm not allowed on the seat, but I jump up on it anyway so that I can look out the window. I went in Cyril's car once to go to the vet and I was able to get my whole head out the window. The feeling of the wind was wonderful. It felt like white-water rafting and rappelling and flying all at once. Not that I think I've done any of those things.

The conductor comes by, and I jump off the seat and hide under the table at Pip's feet.

"You got a ticket?" he asks.

I bet he thinks Pip can't afford a ticket.

"Yes," Pip says, proudly showing it to him. I feel proud of Pip too.

The train stops several times before we get out.

"End of the line!" someone shouts, and we all tumble out onto the platform.

Chapter 7

This place is by the ocean. I can smell the sea air and it puts a spring in my step.

"It's a little late to make phone calls now, Ray," Pip says to me. "But we'll find a pay phone and start in the morning. We'd better find somewhere to sleep."

There is a pier and a long boardwalk by the beach. Down on the sand there is a food truck. Pip has just enough money for fries and a hot dog. He saves all his change for the phone. We sit on the beach and watch the waves breaking against the shore. Pip gives me half his hot dog and some of his fries.

"Things'll get better, don't you worry," he says.

But I *am* worried. I'm worried that Pip won't be able to find his dad and then he'll be taken back to his foster parents. I wouldn't be allowed to visit him *there*. I decide that if I can help it, I won't ever let Pip out of my sight. But before that I just have to run along the shore.

A breeze has blown up now. The beach is becoming deserted and we wander back into town. We walk down side streets and across squares until we come to the back of a huge hotel. There is a grate in the pavement with hot air blowing out of it.

"Here we are, Ray. We'll sleep here for the night."

Pip takes out his sleeping bag and an old towel for me to sleep on. It's quite warm by the grate, but there's a chill in the air. I give Pip's face a lick. It tastes salty. I can see a big tear rolling down his cheek.

"I miss Mom," he whispers, and makes room

for me in his sleeping bag. I crawl in next to him and rest my chin on his hand.

We are woken early by seagulls screaming at a trash truck. We go back to the beach. I look in the barrels that the garbagemen haven't emptied yet. I'm surprised Pip doesn't want any of it. There's tons of good stuff in here. I hastily eat a potato skin and a stale muffin. Really, I can't imagine why I was so disgusted by trash. It's a positive *haven* of things to eat. Even if it's just licking something off a paper bag.

When we get to the beach Pip throws stones into the ocean. He makes them skim across the top of the water. I can still remember my dream about Jack and wonder if he's out there somewhere in a big wooden ship with acres of sails. I see another dog on the sand and run off to chase it. Then the dog chases me, and before we know it there are three or four other dogs all chasing one another. I hear Pip call, "Ray! Come on!"

The other dogs know it's not a call for them and keep on running around in circles. I'm proud that

Pip is calling for me and I show off by sprinting very fast across the sand, shouting as I go.

"I'm here! Wait for me! Don't leave me!"

We are trying to find the library. There are so many things I have to get a good sniff at on the way. Simply tons of dogs I've never met and probably never will have left me messages on the lampposts and mailboxes. They don't usually say more than "Hi! I was here and this is *my* lamppost." Sometimes it's someone looking for a mate. It's a little like being on Facebook. It doesn't matter that it's not a worldwide web. It's small and intimate and how I like it. I want to leave a few messages as well, but I'm not letting Pip out of my sight, so I can only leave one or two.

My vow to not let Pip out of my sight is short-lived. We find the local library and I have to let him go in alone.

It's surprising how many people stop and talk to a dog on its own. I don't think anyone stops to talk to Pip. Except for the couple of men who wanted to talk to him about Jesus.

So far ten people have patted me. Two people

have asked me if I'm dangerous and will I bite them. And one person has given me the crust of her sandwich.

At last Pip comes out of the library with a piece of paper on which he's written some numbers.

"There are four Seagroves!" he says excitedly, and we leave to find a phone.

I jump up and down at his side. "Well done, Pip! Well done!" I say as we race along the pavement. "Perhaps they're *all* related to you!"

The first three pay phones we find only take cards or only dial emergency numbers.

"But this *is* an emergency," I say. "You should be able to ask the emergency services to find your dad."

I'm not sure Pip is listening.

"Shhh, Ray. I'm trying to think," he says.

Now we're at a phone that takes coins, and I can see Pip dialing the first number. There is no one there, just an answering machine. Pip hangs up and tries another number. I can hear it ringing. It is in time with my heartbeat, which seems to have quickened with anticipation. A voice is at the other end.

"Hello," says Pip. "Does Phillip Seagrove live there?"

I thought *he* was Phillip Seagrove. I feel confused. I guess he has the same name as his dad. I can hear the voice at the other end say, "No. No one of that name here." And then the sound of the dial tone again.

The third number has a *number not in service* message on it. Pip gets an answer on the fourth.

"*Phillip* Seagrove?" the voice says. "No, I'm *Daphne* Seagrove."

"Are you related, maybe?" asks Pip. "Do you *know* a Phillip Seagrove?"

"Now, let me think," the voice says. "I think my mother may have had a cousin called Phillip. But he wouldn't have been a Seagrove, of course. Anyway, he'd be dead by now. I'm nearly ninety! You wouldn't think it, would you? Perhaps it was Patrick, not Phillip. Sorry, dear, I can't help you." And the line goes dead. Pip sighs.

"OK, Ray. Two out of four, voice mail, and a number not in service. We'll have to try again, but I'm out of money."

He seems disheartened. We are back at the grate behind the hotel again. There are a couple of men already there with bottles of cider. They seem harmless enough, but Pip won't let me check them out. We've found some expired sandwiches behind a corner store.

"It's my birthday tomorrow, Ray," Pip says as he hands me a ham sandwich. "This is my first birthday without Mom. She always made me a birthday cake. Chocolate, usually, because that's my favorite. She gave me this watch last year."

He takes a watch out of his bag.

"It's lovely," I tell him. "It even has a date on it, doesn't it?"

I'm trying to think of *my* last birthday, but I can't even remember if I *had* a cake. When I think of it, it's like there is an empty space in my memory where my birthday used to be. And if I think too hard about it, there's a sort of buzzing sensation in my mind, like an angry insect is guarding the empty space from the memory.

In the morning I cover him with kisses.

"Happy birthday, Pip," I say to him. If I were a cat, I would go off and catch him a little mouse as a present. But what can I give him?

We go to the beach. There's no one on it and the tide is beginning to come in. There is a line of plastic bottles and seaweed and bits of driftwood and bits of fishing nets and empty crab shells. All good to sniff at. Pip puts down his bag and begins to take off his jacket.

"I've just got to go and have a swim. It's tradition, you see. I always have this urge to go into water on my birthday. My mom used to say I was trying to get back into the womb."

"But it's too cold to swim now. What if you get a cramp?" I say to him.

There is a shoe washed up with the seaweed and I go and fetch it. I start running around him with it in my mouth and drop it in front of him. I don't want him going in the water. I think it's too

115

dangerous. When I see he's not going to throw the shoe, I go and fetch a piece of the driftwood.

"Come on, Ray, just sit here by my clothes and guard the bag."

I look around me. In the distance I can see a figure walking, but it is a long way away. Otherwise it doesn't seem as if there is anyone on the beach. Pip takes off all his clothes except his underpants and then runs into the surf.

"Come back!" I shout.

He dives into the waves and disappears from sight. I get up, anxious that he won't surface again, but there he is a little farther out, grinning and waving at me. He starts swimming. He is a strong swimmer and soon he is far out.

"Come back!" I shout again. I leave the bag and run along the shoreline. How can I keep an eye on him if he swims so far out? My paws are wet now. It's not as cold as I thought it would be, so I run farther in. But Pip is swimming farther and farther away.

I start to swim after him and shout at him to stop and be careful and watch what he's doing. The current is strong, and although I am swimming straight at him, I can feel I am being swept farther down along the beach. How am I going to rescue him and bring him back to safety if he keeps swimming away?

Pip's bag looks a long way away now. And so does Pip. A big wave sweeps over my head and sucks me down. I'm caught up in it and my body is turning over and over and I'm not sure which way is up. I'm holding my breath, but I can feel it leaving my body, and my lungs ache now. I've got my eyes open to see which way is up, but the water is cloudy with lots of grit and sand flying past.

At last I bob up to the surface. My paws are paddling hard to keep me above the water. I look around me. Pip's bag is now a speck on the beach, and it looks as if he is standing by it, because I can see a figure bending down.

Good. I can relax a little. I can stop worrying about both Pip and his bag. But then I hear a shout and there is Pip *swimming toward me.*

Another wave gets hold of me and hurls me onto the shore.

"Ray! You silly dog. You didn't have to come in after me. I was coming back."

"But Pip!" I choke, spitting the seaweed out of my mouth. "Who's with the bag?"

Although I know Pip doesn't understand me, something causes him to look along the beach, and we both see someone making off with Pip's bag.

"Oh, no!" He curses and starts to run up the beach. "Everything I own is in that bag. It's all I have."

I struggle to my feet and run after him, but the weight of the water in my fur slows me down. I have to stop and shake it off and I lose valuable seconds. This really is all my fault. If only I had stayed with the bag and not been so eager to keep up with Pip. He was right. I am a silly dog.

It's a man who has the bag and he's walking fast along the beach with it tucked under his arm.

"Stop! That's my bag!" yells Pip.

The man turns for a moment and then quickens his pace. There is still quite a gap between us. I am now running flat out. I'm faster than Pip and determined to get the bag, even though I remember it's got my leash in it. It has Pip's watch in it as well, and I want him to always know when his birthday is. I can't remember mine anymore.

The man with the bag is running now, but he is not sure on his feet and stumbles on the stones.

"Come back with that bag!" I yell. "It doesn't belong to you and it's got Pip's whole world in it!"

But the man gets up and keeps running. He is wearing loose pants and the hems are flapping as he runs. All my muscles are working and I feel as if I am eating up the distance between us. I am close enough now and I get ready to leap. I spring from my back legs and I soar through the air. The force of my jump pulls my mouth back, and with a snap of my teeth I get hold of his pants. My jaws may not be good for bubblegum, but they certainly work when you want to get hold of a pant leg.

There is a ripping sound and the man falls onto the sand. I see a bare ankle and I fasten my teeth on it. He smells stale, of alcohol and fear.

The man yells out, "Get that crazy dog off me!" And Pip races up to my side. He grabs the bag off the man before he says to me, "That's enough, Ray. Leave him."

Reluctantly I let go of the man's ankle. He scrambles up. He has a wild look in his eyes and a tattoo of a snake winding around his neck. I back off. There's something about the snake I don't like, and although I know it's not real, I'm going to keep my distance now in case it suddenly comes alive.

"I thought it had been left. I thought it didn't belong to no one." He has a thin, whiny voice and he backs away from us, looking for somewhere to run.

"Well it does!" yells Pip. "It belongs to me. Go away and leave us alone or I'll sic my dog on you again!"

At this I show him my teeth and I shout at him, "Yes! Clear off and leave us alone!"

He's running now, back up the beach, not fast, because he's limping a bit. I look at Pip and wag my tail.

"Good Ray!" says Pip. I like it when he praises me, and I put my ears flat back so that he can stroke my head. I feel much braver about the snake now.

We go back to where Pip's clothes are, and he takes the picture of his dad out of his pocket and looks at it. I realize that this is the most important thing he has. Apart from me, that is.

We follow in the footsteps of the man and I have a good sniff at his prints. I still have the image of his snake and half expect to find its track on the sand as well. All that seawater I swallowed must be playing tricks with my mind. It's not a big town, and I hope we don't see him again. Even with my newfound braveness, I'm not sure I could fight off more than one person if he happened to have some friends. This is going to give me something else to worry about.

There's something fluttering along the sand in front of us. I run to catch it. It's a folded-up piece of paper. I pick it up to show Pip. Neither Pip nor I can stand people throwing litter on the ground. It brings out the policewoman in me.

"What's this, Ray?" he says, taking the paper out of my mouth.

"Gosh!" he says. 'It's a twenty-dollar bill!"

He dances around me and I join in.

"Twenty bucks! What a fantastic birthday present, Ray! Good job!"

My tail is now going around and around like a propeller and I think I might take off. This is better than presenting him with a little mouse.

"I think that man dropped it when he was running away. I bet he stole it from someone else. Like he took our bag," I tell him.

Pip looks around.

"There's no one to give it back to. So I think we'll *have* to keep it. *Happy birthday, Pip!*" he shouts.

"Happy birthday, Pip!" I shout back.

We run along the beach and back into town.

"We'll have to buy something so I can get more change for the telephone," he says. Then I can see his eyes light up. "And I know just what it's going to be!"

I follow him up the side streets. There's a lovely smell coming from a shop a few doors along.

"Stay here, Ray," Pip says as he goes inside.

I look into the shop. It is full of loaves of bread and pastries, and smells absolutely delicious. In a few minutes Pip comes out carrying a white box tied up with ribbon.

"Come on! Back to the beach!" he yells to me, and we retrace our footsteps and go and sit under the pier and Pip opens the box and inside is a beautiful chocolate cake.

Chapter 8

When Pip gets through to the voice-mail number a man with a thick foreign accent answers.

"Hello," says Pip, speaking slowly and rather loudly in case the man doesn't understand him. "Does Phillip Seagrove live there?"

There is a pause on the other end of the line.

"No. Very sorry. Mr. Seagrove passed away a year now."

Pip catches his breath and says, "Oh, no! That can't be. How can he die when I haven't found him yet?"

I'm not sure if he's talking to himself or the man on the phone, but the voice on the other end continues.

"Well," the voice says, "he was very old and had been ill some time."

"How old?" asks Pip.

"I am thinking eighty-something."

Pip sighs with relief.

"Oh, not *my* Mr. Seagrove, then. Did he have a son, do you think?"

"Oh, no, no. Mr. Seagrove, he having no family. I had to make all arrangement for him."

"I am sorry," says Pip. "But thank you."

He looks pleased until he realizes he is still no closer to finding his father. He tries the disconnected line again and gets the same recorded message.

"You know what, Ray? We're going to go around to the address in the phone book, just in case the number has been changed."

The address is on Barton Road.

"Let's find a map," says Pip, excited again.

I'm excited too. I want Pip to find his dad. I'm trying to picture *my* dad now.

He has a hat and coat and no face and a car with a license plate number that I cannot possibly remember.

Barton Road is up a long hill and full of white-washed houses. When we get to the top we look back over the bay. There are a few fishing boats and someone water-skiing. It's practically winter and I tell Pip that I think the water-skier must be nuts. He'd be sure to get hypothermia if he fell in.

Number ten has a little front gate and a well-tended front yard. Pip waits outside for a while.

"Go on, Pip," I say. "Go and knock on the door."

"I'm feeling nervous, Ray. What if he answers the door? I wish I could have spoken to him on the phone first. What if he doesn't believe I'm his son?"

Then Pip pauses a moment and adds, "What if we don't like each other?"

I tell him I'm sure they will and search my brain for any clues that I liked *my* father. But my memory seems blocked and I can't even remember what he did for a living.

We've been hanging around the gate for some time now. I notice a woman with white hair by the curtains, looking at us.

"Go *on*, Pip," I say.

"Be quiet, Ray. You'll disturb the neighbors."

But too late now. The door opens and the woman appears.

"Can I help you, dear?" she says. "Are you looking for someone?"

"Yes," says Pip. "Does Phillip Seagrove live here?"

"Ah, no," the woman replies, and I know Pip's heart has sunk, just like mine. "But I still have a forwarding address, I think, if you just hang on a moment."

She goes back into the house and is gone for some time. Pip shifts his weight from foot to foot. Takes his hands out of his pockets, then puts them in again. Then takes them out. He opens and shuts the gate several times.

"Sorry about that," says the woman when she returns with a piece of paper. "It was at the back of one of the drawers. They moved out about a year ago now." She hands Pip the paper.

"*They?*" he says.

"Yes. A really nice family. They have a little boy."

I notice Pip stiffen.

"Any dogs?" I ask.

The woman strokes me. "Are you being ignored? I had a dog like you once, with those colored eyes. A collie called Jessie."

"Was she a spirit dog?" I ask. But the lady is on her way back inside.

"Where is this?" Pip calls out.

"It's just along the coast, dear. Not too far! Good luck!"

Pip turns the paper over in his hands.

"Well, Ray. Looks as if we might find him after all." But I can tell he's not as happy as I thought he'd be.

We walk off down the road and I wonder if Pip knows where we are going.

Pip's still got change from the twenty and

128

suggests we go into a café and have something to eat. We pass one now. There is a tantalizing smell of beef cooking on a big stove and a lasagna that has just been taken out of the oven.

"Lasagna!" I say. "My favorite, after . . . well." That busy insect is back again, daring me to remember my other favorite dishes. I give up and sniff at a lamppost.

"Come on, Ray, let's have something to eat."

"You can't bring that dog in here," says the man cutting up the lasagna.

"OK," Pip says, sounding disappointed. "We'll go, then."

I want to say to him that it doesn't matter. I'm quite happy to sit outside the café. I want him to have something to eat because I worry he's not getting enough vitamins. I'm beginning to sound like my mom. But Mom's face doesn't come to mind as it used to, and all I get is a glimpse of an apron with I'M THE BOSS written on it.

I suddenly feel weary and don't see the point of telling Pip all this if he can't understand what I'm saying.

"We do takeout!" the man says as we start to leave the café.

We are sitting on some rocks under the pier, sharing the lasagna.

"You know, Ray," Pip tells me, in between mouthfuls, "I've been thinking of Dad for all this time, since Mom died, and I don't know what I imagined, but I hadn't thought of him with another family. I thought he'd be on his own, like me, and that he'd be happy to have the company. Now I'm afraid he won't want us because he'll be too busy with his other family. And what if his wife doesn't like me? She'll probably be mad he got another woman pregnant before her."

I rest my head in his lap and look up at him.

"It'll be fine, Pip. He won't turn you away." I want to add that he may turn *me* away. What if they have a dog like that jealous Moss? Two dogs is one dog too many. But I keep that to myself.

We spend our night behind the hotel. There is quite a gathering of people there now and it's noisy. Pip and I curl up together. I dream of the man with the tattoo. I dream that the snake uncoils itself from around the man's neck and slithers after me. I try to run, but in my dream I've eaten too much lasagna and cannot move. The snake flicks out its tongue and bites me in the stomach.

I wake up with a yelp and a feeling that my belly is on fire. Pip is not in good shape either, and he has his knees up on his chest and is moaning softly. He looks rather ashen. He sees me looking at him.

"I feel *awful*, Ray. I want to be sick but I can't with all these people around. I think I need some fresh air. Let's move down to the pier."

There is no one around as we make our way slowly to the beach. Pip is bent double most of the way and continues to moan to himself. He throws up a few times behind a rock. I'm sick in some seaweed and feel much better after. I decide that lasagna is no longer my favorite food.

Pip splashes seawater on his face and then drags his things up the beach, gets his sleeping bag out, and gets in it. There is an overwhelming smell of rotting fish and seaweed, but he doesn't seem to care. I lick his face to make him feel better, but he's got his eyes shut now. I think of Jack when he was ill. How can *I* get pills for Pip?

I stay with him and watch the sunrise. A few early-morning walkers arrive on the beach, but we are hidden from view, and when I get up and look back at Pip in his sleeping bag, he just looks like another rock.

I decide to get help. There is a jogger coming along the beach. I run toward him.

"Can you help us?" I say. "My Pip is ill and I think he needs a doctor or to go to the hospital or something."

The jogger has earphones in and is listening to music. I don't think he can hear me. I jump up at him as he's running along, but he just kicks out at me and waves his arms.

"Shooooo!" he says, and puts on a spurt of speed. I want to nip his stupid Lycra-clad legs. I won't help *him* if he's ever in trouble. I watch him run and think how ridiculous humans look sometimes.

I try a couple of other people, but they think I want to play with them and throw things into the ocean for me. I'm too polite to ignore them, so I go and fetch the things back, but I can't get them to follow me. What should I do? I shout my frustration at the waves and begin to make my way back to Pip. He looks very pale and seems to be asleep. I hope he's not dead. I put my nose near his mouth and feel my whiskers tickled by his breath. At least he's alive. But what am I going to do?

I remember the nice old lady who gave us Pip's dad's address. She's the only person we've had contact with in this town. Surely if I could find her house again, she would come and help Pip.

But I am torn. How can I leave him? What if something happens to him while I am away? What if he wakes up and finds I'm gone? He might be feeling better and get up and go, and then I might never see him again. I sit down next to him and wait.

After a while I think I'll try to wake him.

"Pip," I say, nudging him gently. "I think I'd better go and get some help."

Pip opens his eyes and stares at me. I don't think he knows who I am.

"Pip! It's me. Ray. I'm going to go and get that lady who lives in your dad's old house."

"Why are you whining at me?" Pip slurs. "I can't come and play with you. I feel too sick. Can't you find another dog to play with?" And he pulls his sleeping bag up over his ears and goes back to sleep.

Well, that's that, then. I'm going to have to find the old lady. I'll just have to hope he doesn't move before I come back.

I retrace our steps. Back to the grate outside the hotel. Back to the spot on the beach where we ate. I can hardly bring myself to think of what we ate in case I'm sick again. I know this is a backward way of doing it, but I can't remember the route to the restaurant unless I do *exactly* what we did the night before. Anyway, we didn't sit on this exact same spot of the beach, so I don't feel quite so silly.

From the beach I take another route. I can smell the café from around the corner. Breakfast.

Spoiled bacon and soggy toast. I feel like telling them they ought to be closed down for food poisoning, but I'm in a hurry.

Then where did we come from? I remember we ambled a bit and I didn't think that Pip knew where we were going. Why do all these roads look the same? Barton Road! Where are you?

I steer clear of the newspaper boy. I'd like to ask him the way, but I know what will happen, so I keep going. And I'm not stopping to sniff anything either, even though quite a few dogs have already been out, even this early in the morning.

Thank goodness I can still read. After a false alarm with a Barnaby Road, I see the sign.

I race up the sidewalk and reach the gate. What now? Old ladies probably sleep late. She's probably deaf too and may not sleep with her hearing aid in. Nevertheless. Time is not on my side. I jump up and over the wall.

"Wake up! Wake up! I need help here. Come to the door and you'll see who it is!"

I jump up against the gate, willing it to fall open.

"Stop that wretched barking!" A man in pajamas pulls down the window of the house next door. "Some of us are trying to sleep!"

But I keep going. I have to get her attention. And I do.

I was expecting her to be wearing her nightie, but she is fully dressed.

"Hello! It's *you*! Where's your friend? That nice boy you were with?"

"He's sick. Very sick. Could you help me, please? If you follow me I'll show you where he is, because I don't really know what to do. We ate some bad lasagna from a café last night and although I haven't been feeling too good, Pip is much worse than me."

"Can't you shut that dog up?" The man in pajamas is back at his window again.

"Sorry, Mr. Pettigrew." The old lady looks up. "I'll take him inside with me."

"I'm a girl, actually, not a boy," I say. "I can't come in the house. You've got to follow me. Please come! He's very sick. He needs help." I run around in circles, trot a little way to the gate, and go back to her side. I repeat this several times.

"Oh dear, oh dear. What's the matter? Has something happened?" She looks up at Mr. Pettigrew's window. "Won't be a minute!" she calls up to him. "I think the dog's a bit upset."

She turns back to me.

"Oh, dear. I don't know what to do. I think you're trying to tell me something, aren't you?"

I wag my tail at her encouragingly.

"Is it that you want me to follow you?"

"Yes!" I bark.

The wonderful woman gets her coat and follows me down the road. I go back to her every now and then to make sure she is still coming. We go onto the beach and I race over to the rocks. Pip is just where I left him, with his eyes still shut.

"Oh, you poor boy," she says when she sees him. "What's happened?"

I lick Pip's face and he opens his eyes. They look red and watery. I don't think he realizes it's the woman we went to see, but he manages to speak and tells her he's eaten something bad.

"Well, my boy," she says, "you'd better come back with me and I'll see what I can do. Can you walk a little way? No, perhaps not. If you stay here with your dog I'll go back and get my car. If you can manage to get to it, I can drive you back home and you can lie on a real bed. I've got some very good medicine for food poisoning. Will you be all right for a short while? I'm Marjorie, by the way."

Chapter 9

Marjorie's house is warm and comfortable and simply packed with pictures of her dog, Jessie. I look into the dog's eyes in a framed photo and I see my eyes staring back.

"You can sleep on her old blanket if you like," she says to me. "For some reason I've kept it, and her travel bed is still in my car. Silly of me, really, isn't it? I'll put the blanket down in front of the fire, and Pip, you can have the bed in the spare room." She makes him comfortable and gives him her very good medicine and pours me a bowl of milk.

"It's been a long time since I've had a dog lie in front of that fire. I miss Jessie, you know, Ray. She understood everything I said to her. Like I get the feeling *you* do. Is that right?"

I wag my tail.

"Did she frighten farm animals?" I ask her. But she just smiles at me and looks after Pip.

"You and Ray best stay here for a while, Pip, to get your strength up before starting your journey. I am planning on driving you there myself, if you like. To spare you the traveling. I don't go out in the car much, and a little journey in the country will do me and the car some good."

Relief seems to flood over Pip's face. I wag my tail at him. Marjorie's going to make him better, I know.

Pip sleeps for two days. He tosses and turns, and I watch his color change from very pale to warm pink again. I don't tell Marjorie in case she thinks I'm ungrateful, but when she goes to bed I lie outside Pip's door in case he needs me.

Marjorie takes me for early-morning walks before breakfast while Pip is still recovering, and I trot along happily at her side, knowing he is getting well. She is very tolerant and doesn't seem to mind me stopping every so often to find out who's been around.

"I can't see the point in sleeping my life away, Ray," she tells me as we walk along the road. "I probably don't have long now. I'm really quite old." She bends down and gives me a pat. "I'm not afraid of dying, you know."

I want to tell her about the Job Center and the woman behind the desk and to make sure she goes through the wrong door if she wants to remember who she is, but I can't put it into words for her. So I just wag my tail.

"When my husband passed away, I got Jessie as a puppy from a farmer. He didn't want her on his farm. So she came with me."

I like this story. It means there are probably lots of dogs like me out there, with strange eyes. And the farmer probably didn't want her because his cows were freaked out by her eyes. I want to believe Jack's story of spirit dogs.

"My husband never really liked dogs and would

never let me have one when he was alive. Actually, he was a very grumpy person. He hardly ever spoke to me. And I had no one to talk to. When Jessie came along it was quite a different story. It was just like having another person living with me, but one who enjoyed my company, never criticized me, and was always happy to see me!"

I think of Jack and how nice it would be if he and Marjorie could be together. I think they would have a lot to talk about. But how could I tell her about this old man a train journey away, who may not even be alive?

We stay with Marjorie for a week. Pip plays cards with her at night and we all settle down together on her sofa to watch television. It's been ages since I've seen a television. I particularly like the wildlife shows. I think neither of us has ever eaten so well either. Marjorie makes yummy casseroles for Pip and gives me the gravy, with some biscuits, for dinner.

Then one day Pip decides it's time we went on our way. He has the address of his father burning a hole in his pocket, I think, and can wait no longer. He finally tells Marjorie his whole story. She puts her arms around him.

"I'm determined to drive you there, dear. I don't want you having to tramp the streets again." Marjorie goes out to check the oil and gas in her car and minutes later comes back in, looking flustered.

"My car is gone! Where my car was is an empty space! I can't think what's happened to it."

"Do you think you parked it somewhere else and have forgotten where?" asks Pip.

"Well, dear, I don't think so. When I parked it I remember thinking the passenger door was a bit near the lamppost. The lamppost is still there—but not my car! There's been a spate of car thefts recently. I'd better tell the police."

Pip is worried about the police seeing him and taking him back to the foster parents and says he better hide somewhere if they come around.

"Well, dear, if you're really worried I'll call the police after you've gone. So, as I can't drive you, I'm going to give you my old bicycle. I expect the tires need pumping up. I don't use it anymore.

It's mainly country lanes to get to your father's, so you should be all right. Is that a good idea?"

Pip nods and I'm thrilled. It means lots of things to sniff at on the way and a chance to really stretch my legs. Pip pumps up the tires and Marjorie gives him a pack of sandwiches.

"There's a little something for you as well, Ray."

"Thank you, thank you!" I say to her. "You've been so kind and saved my Pip. I hope you get another dog one day."

"Ah, my dears!" she says. "It's been lovely knowing you. Don't forget to come and visit if you're this way again." And she strokes my head and hugs Pip, and we set off down the road.

There is a wintry sun out and I'm excited. Pip flashes me a grin as he coasts down the hill. We are soon out of the town and in open country. I keep on the inside of Pip when we are on a busy stretch of road, but as soon as we get to the quiet roads I'm all over the place. There is so much to smell. Simply loads of animals have been along the lanes. A badger has been here, a fox has left his scent there, and I nearly catch a pheasant that is pecking by the roadside. Really, they are such stupid birds. I'm glad I didn't come back as a *pheasant*. If they didn't draw attention to themselves by flapping their wings and screeching you wouldn't notice them half the time. This one is so fat it can hardly get up into the air, and I manage to grab one of its tail feathers before it finally takes off. I give the feather to Pip and he puts it in his hat.

Sometimes I get left behind a little if there is a particularly good smell, but Pip calls my name and it's my chance to tear along the road and make my ears fly. We stop for sandwiches. Marjorie has put in those little bone-shaped biscuits for me. How happy I am to see them! It's funny what you take for granted. I wasn't too pleased with them at Cyril's, but I haven't seen them in so long I eat them excitedly. The last one I had was outside my old house on Alexander Avenue. I realize I can remember everything as a dog with great clarity, but when I try to picture my bedroom I have absolutely no idea what it looked like. I just have some vague memory of a swirling pink net.

We continue along the road. Suddenly a hare runs out in front of Pip's bicycle. He wobbles and I think falls off the bike, but I'm after the hare before I've had time to think. How *dare* it cause my Pip to fall off the bike? What does it think it's doing? And it hasn't even stopped to see if Pip is all right. And although I haven't stopped to see if Pip is all right either, I'm off to have words with it.

It's gone through a hedge and out the other side and I have too. It's the fastest thing I've ever chased, and every time I think I'm nearly on it, it zigzags across the field and I've lost valuable seconds. I think I can hear Pip's voice calling me, but my concentration is on catching the hare and I can't possibly stop now. I think I really am flying again. My paws hardly touch the ground. There is stubble in this field that pricks my paws when I do touch down, but the next has been plowed. The one after is rough grass and then I lose the hare! Where has it gone? There is a big crater in the middle of the field filled with brambles and old, rusty pieces of farm machinery, and the hare has gone to ground somewhere in it, I'm now sure. I spend ages sniffing around for it and then finally give up.

I suddenly remember Pip. Where is he? I scan the horizon and all I can see is fields. No road. No bike. I've probably been gone forever. I don't seem to have any sense of time anymore. I try to run back the way I came, but I'm panting so much now that I've stopped I can only manage a limping trot. My tongue is hanging out as far as I can get it and I'm trying to catch my breath too. I cross the plowed field, but I'm not sure which stubble field I've crossed. There seem to be a lot of them. And now a wind has blown up and if Pip *were* calling me I wouldn't stand a chance of hearing him.

I begin to panic. How can I have been so stupid as to chase that hare? How can I have left Pip after my vow never to let him out of my sight? And the more I think about the hare, the more I realize that the instincts of being a dog are taking over the instincts of being Daisy. And it scares me.

I haven't a clue where I am now. I see a road winding its way between some fields in the distance and make my way toward it. With any luck it'll be Pip's road. To get to it I have to go through a hedge and over a ditch, and as I emerge I see something big and metal poking out of the hedge on the other side. I cross the road to check it out. It's a car with its back wheels in the ditch and its front wheels through the hedge. I wonder if there is someone still in the car, but the door is open and I can't smell anyone around. I look inside. On the backseat is a dog bed. A red-and-black-checked bed. I remember Marjorie telling me that she still kept Jessie's travel bed in her car. This is definitely Marjorie's missing car!

I really want to tell Marjorie where her car is, but I'm not exactly sure I know. I am hoping this is the road Pip is on, but has he passed the car or not reached it yet? He probably won't know what Marjorie's car looks like, he was so ill when he traveled in it. And now it's beginning to rain!

Big fat drops are falling on me. *Pitter. Patter.* I hate getting wet. So I jump into Marjorie's car and try to settle down.

Someone's been in the car who doesn't smell good.

I feel my hackles begin to rise. The smell reminds me of being on the beach. Yes! That's it. *The snake man.* This car definitely smells like him!

I get up at once and carefully look under the seats in case he's still in the car and hiding.

He's not there.

I put my nose into the travel bed. Yes, there's Marjorie's dog's smell — I remember it from the blanket in the house. Very faint, because it must have been ages since she lay on this bed. She smells like a kind dog. Caramel and wool. She smells like she was a good age. I settle down on the red-and-black bed and wait for Pip.

Oh dear, poor Pip — he is going to be soaked through by now. If only he could get here quickly and take shelter in the car. I hear thunder in the distance and I shiver. I've never liked thunderstorms, and now that I'm a dog I seem to hate them even more. I can't stop my body from shaking and I'm whimpering and fretting now, which I find a bit pathetic, but I can't control it. What if Pip meets the snake man on the road? The wind has begun to shriek through the trees.

The rain is absolutely pouring down and banging on the roof. It's like being inside a tin drum. *Clatter, clatter, thud, thud.* I don't want Pip to catch a chill. I strain my ears for the whirr of a bicycle wheel but nothing passes. I can hear the gasp of a mouse in the hedgerow, though, and the high-pitched whine of some flying insect. This hearing thing is fantastic.

Eventually the storm blows over and a watery afternoon sun pokes out from behind the clouds. There is a hushed stillness. I get out of Marjorie's car and decide to continue along the road to look for Pip. It's a quiet road and only one or two cars have passed me going the other way. A blue van passes me, splashing me with a puddle. *Swish. Swoosh. Squelch. Squeal.* It slams on its brakes a little way in front of me. A woman gets out.

Now, the Daisy part of me issues a warning.

Don't talk to strangers and never get into a car with someone you don't know. But the dog part of me is pleased to see someone, and my tail just wags all on its own.

"Hello, little dog," the woman says, holding out her hand. "Ain't you got no home? You're a fine dog, ain't you? Who do you belong to, then?"

A man gets out of the van and shouts to her. "Don't it belong to no one?"

She strokes my head and reads the tag on my collar.

"Ray and Pip. Don't seem to have no number or address. Don't know if the dog is Ray *or* Pip. But it looks like a stray to me. We might as well take it. Come on—I've got a nice treat for you in the van."

I obediently follow her. I can see no point in telling her I'm not a stray and, after all, we might pass Pip on the way. Besides, I'm feeling a bit hungry now that I've stopped all that panting.

I jump into the van and the woman gives me a gingersnap. The van smells of cigarettes and faraway places. I give it a full examination and then settle down in the front so that I can look out the window.

We drive along the road at various speeds. When the man is lighting a cigarette he slows down and when he's finished he speeds up. I feel like telling him he shouldn't smoke. That by smoking he's shortening his life and ours by being in the van with him. But I don't feel like chatting. I'm keeping an eye out for Pip.

After a while they begin to argue about Marjorie's car and whether or not they should tell the police they've seen a car in the ditch. Then the man turns up the radio and some loud music blares out. I don't like it and busy myself looking out the window. I want them to roll it down so that I can get my head out, but the man's put the heater on and I suppose they don't want to sit in a draft.

We drive along, the man tapping his hands on the steering wheel in time to the music and the woman singing to herself. As we go around a bend in the road I see a bicycle ahead.

"Stop! Stop the van! It's Pip! There he is! On

the bicycle. Let me out. I belong to Pip. I must get to him." I am scratching at the door now, trying to get out.

"What's that dog barking for?" says the man. "Shut that barking up, will you?"

But I'm not going to give up that easily. I am desperate now. The van passes Pip on the bicycle. "Stop! Stop! Let me *out*!"

I race from one side of the van to the other, making as much noise as possible. The man is beginning to look angry.

Pip is riding furiously along the road. I'm not sure if he's seen me. If only I could have gotten my head out the window. I'm in this blue van and he doesn't know. I feel as if part of me is lost without him and I'm pretty sure he is feeling the same thing. He's probably calling my name, hoping I can hear. But I can't, because the radio is on and I can't do anything about it. I start to wail. Long, painful sobs that echo around the inside of the van.

"We shouldn't have picked that dog up," says the man, taking his eyes off the road to look at me.

"Aw—why not? He's a nice doggie. He'll shut up sooner or later—won't you, PipRay?"

But I continue to whine and we keep on driving, getting farther and farther away from my Pip.

Then I hear a new noise. *Fizz. Sizzle. Splutter. Seethe. Sigh.* The van starts to bump and veer into the center of the road.

"Blast!" says the driver. "We've got a flat! Why do you always get a flat when it's wet?"

He pulls to the side of the road and turns off the engine.

"I've got a jack in the back," he says, and I hear him coming around to the rear door. I'm ready. I know there will only be a second before his frame fills the gap left when he opens the door. *Click.* The handle turns and I fly out. Launching myself into the gray space. I hit the road at a run. I'm not hanging around to be caught again. I can hear the woman cry out and the man say, "Aw, let him go. He makes too much noise."

And I race back the way we've come.

"Pip! Pip!" I'm shouting. "It's me! Ray!" I am tearing along, ignoring the rabbits that scuttle back into the hedgerow and the crow pecking at something dead in the road. And there in the distance is a little figure riding through the puddles and it's my dear Pip. When he sees me he drops his bike and I run toward him and he runs toward me and we're in each other's arms.

"I thought I'd never see you again, Ray." He covers me in kisses and wipes his nose. I look at him and I see he's been crying.

Chapter 10

We are on top of a hill now and looking down on the town where Pip's dad lives. People are turning their lights on and shafts of smoke are rising from the chimneys. I can see quite well at night, better than when I was Daisy. I can make out each building. I can see people in the road. I can see dogs out on walks. I can see a television set flickering in an upstairs room.

"It's too late to try now," says Pip. "We should find somewhere to sleep. I think we'd better stay out here and ride down into town in the morning. Come on. There are some bushes over there we can crawl under."

"I'll keep you warm, Pip," I tell him, and we make our camp under the bush and I turn around and around for him to make sure there are no snakes hiding and to make it really comfy for him. We eat the remains of Marjorie's sandwiches and the last little bone-biscuit.

We have a restless night. I think Pip has a nightmare, because he's talking in his sleep and making groaning noises. I lick his nose to reassure him that everything is all right.

When we get down to the town in the morning, we see some bathrooms by the beach and Pip goes in and washes and brushes his hair and teeth. Marjorie has washed his clothes, and in spite of a night sleeping outside, I think Pip looks really presentable and I feel proud of him. Farther into town we see a newspaper boy outside a shop and Pip asks him where Fielding Road is. I smile at the boy, in case he thinks I'm going to tug on his pants.

We are climbing up a hill again. Fielding Road

is a little like Marjorie's road, and I wonder why Pip's dad bothered to move. Perhaps it's something to do with his work, I think.

"Look, Ray!" says Pip excitedly. "That must be it! The one with the mauve trim and the blue door. It looks like the nicest house on the whole street, doesn't it?"

"Yes," I say positively. "It's a pretty color, isn't it?"

I wonder what Pip is going to do. I'm all for marching straight up and getting it over with. But Pip seems to think otherwise.

"I'm going to wait a bit. See what he looks like."

You know what he looks like. He looks like his picture, I think. But I don't say anything.

We hide the bike behind some bushes farther up the road and stand on the other side of the street behind a parked car. We wait. We wait a long time. I've seen signs of life, curtains and windows opening. I think I see a child's face at a window, but I'm not sure. Then the door opens and a man steps out.

"That's him!" whispers Pip.

I don't think it looks like him at all. His hair isn't that dark color it was in the photo and he doesn't seem to have much of it. Still, he looks nice and that's all that counts.

"Well, go on! Aren't you going to say something?"

"Come on, Ray. Let's follow him. I'm not ready to talk to him yet. He's not expecting us."

The man doesn't seem to have a dog, much to my relief, and he sets off down the hill. He doesn't dawdle and I imagine he has a busy office to get to.

Pip and I follow behind him.

Eventually he turns onto a small street that leads into a busier part of town. The streets are narrower and packed with interesting-looking stores. Lots of places selling books, musical instruments, and Indian crafts. The man stops outside a brightly painted store. Pip looks with interest in the window of the bookshop next door.

The man talks to a girl inside the store as he opens the door.

"Thanks for opening up, Maisie. Sam was sick

and I wanted to let Viv sleep in a bit. She was up with him most of the night."

Through the glass a pretty girl with a pile of pink hair smiles at him.

"That's OK. Is he better now?"

The man shuts the door behind him.

After a while, a delicious smell begins to waft out from the store, and as the street begins to fill up, several people open the door and go in. We creep closer to have a look. It is the most beautifully decorated door, with black-and-white stripes, and above it are the words CAFÉ ZOO.

We stand outside for a good twenty minutes, stepping aside every time someone enters.

"What shall we do?" says Pip. "I feel too nervous to go in, and I've only got fifty cents." But before I can answer him the girl with the pink hair comes to the door.

"Phil says do you want to come in? You can bring your dog if you want."

"Yes, please!" I bark, and wag my tail at her. I'm going to give a good impression so that Pip's father likes me and asks me to stay. Pip hesitates, but I go straight into the café. Maisie strokes my neck.

"Aren't you lovely?" she says. "Phil always keeps a bowl of water down for dogs, don't you, Phil?"

The man we followed down the road nods and smiles.

"What can I get you?" he says to Pip.

A new family! I want him to say, but Pip has become awkward and stutters.

"Uh — w-what can I have for fifty cents?"

"Chocolate brownie and a glass of apple juice sound good to you?"

Pip nods, standing still as if he's glued to the floorboards.

"I'll bring it over to you if you want to go and sit by the window," says Maisie.

The café walls are lined with pictures and paintings of animals, and the tables and chairs have been painted like leopards and tigers and zebras, with spots and stripes. I feel quite at home here. It is warm and I'm enjoying listening to the hum of voices, the coffee machine gurgling on the counter, and Phil or Maisie calling, "Who ordered the Spanish omelet?" or "Hot chocolate, anyone?"

I am lying under the table out of the way, watching Pip's feet tapping up and down. He's nervous and excited, and I wonder when he's going to say something. He makes his brownie last what seems like hours. I wonder what's going through his mind. How's he going to break the news to Phil that he is his son? And what will Phil say? He's already got a son, called Sam, he said. How weird will this be? All these things might be going through Pip's mind. What's going through my mind is whether or not someone will give me something to eat, and the smell of the person who has been at this table before. It's a beachcombing sort of smell. It makes me think of sitting under the pier with Pip, eating our hot dog and fries. Because I can smell fries too. My paws feel sweaty. I realize I'm more nervous than I thought.

The café is busy all morning. People discuss things. Laugh. Exclaim. And it's very loud listening to a lot of people crunching and swallowing their food. There is a gradual changeover from breakfast to lunch, and then it becomes even more busy, with a small line beginning to form outside. Maisie comes over with a cloth and wipes the table. She smiles at Pip.

"Can I get you anything else?"

Pip shakes his head.

"Would you mind if we take your table, then? We're a bit short at the moment."

Pip jumps up immediately.

"Uh . . . sorry," he mumbles, and I also leap to my feet. Is he going to do it now? In front of all these people? But Pip just says "Thank you" to Phil, who lifts a hand in acknowledgment, and we push past the little line and out into the street.

Then Pip starts to run. He's running and skipping and I'm running and skipping and jumping too. "What's going on, Pip?" I say.

"I've got to get some money so that I can go back into the café," he says. "Otherwise I don't know how to see him."

I think Pip's silly. Not that I don't love him — I do. But really, all he has to do is go back to the

163

café, maybe when it's a bit quieter, and tell his dad *who he is.*

"Or we can follow him home again," I say hopefully.

We walk around the town. It's pretty similar to the last one. I think these seaside places were all built by the same person. We find the library. This is obviously where Pip is happiest. And where Pip is happiest, so am I. There is a cardboard box to the side of the building with tattered paperbacks in it. Pip rummages through and produces one. He sits on the steps and reads. I know my job. I lie down, my head on my paws. I follow each passerby with my eyes. If only I could juggle or eat fire or do something *impressive.*

For some time there is nothing in Pip's hat. Then a young man tosses a few coins in. I am waiting for the librarian to come down the steps and ask us to move. But no one disturbs us. A little farther along, a guy is selling a newspaper.

"*Spare Change News,* madam? *Spare Change News,* sir?" I'm happy to see he doesn't have a dog. I'm wondering now, since I can't juggle, if Pip ought to be selling something.

A clock somewhere strikes four and I've had to shut my eyes. I didn't get much sleep under the bush and all the excitement has tired me out. I open them again when I hear a coin land in Pip's hat. I look up. It's the girl with the pink hair from the café.

She smiles at Pip and stops to stroke my head. I can smell coffee and cakes.

"Hello again!" she says.

"Oh, hi!" says Pip.

"You came into the café, didn't you?"

Pip nods.

"I did an early shift today, so Phil's let me go home early. It's nice there, isn't it? Phil's a friend of my mom's and he offered me the job when he first opened up. Did you like the brownie? My mom makes them."

Pip nods and grins at her. I think he likes Maisie. And so do I. She looks kind and has a little silver stud in her nose and chatty earrings.

"What's he like, Phil?" asks Pip, trying to sound casual.

"Oh, he's a great guy. He's so generous and friendly."

"What time does the café close?"

"He closes around six. On Saturdays Mom comes and helps him and we open for supper. It's even busier then. You're new around here, aren't you? Where are you living?"

Pip looks awkward and shrugs.

"There's a youth hostel around the corner if you're looking for somewhere. Go back past the café, cross the main road, and it's the other side of town. I've gotta go. See ya!"

"See ya!" says Pip.

The streetlights are coming on, but everything seems rather dull now that Maisie's gone. Pip picks up his hat, pockets the money, and says to me, "Come on, let's find somewhere to stay. I'll talk to Dad tomorrow."

The café looks as if it's quieting down as we go back past, and Pip and I can't resist a quick look inside. Phil is chatting to a table of customers.

It takes us ages to find the youth hostel, and when we get there the man behind the desk says, "No dogs!"

He doesn't even say sorry!

I know Pip won't leave me, so there's no point in trying to persuade him to stay. Besides, I don't want anyone else to take me home, thinking I'm a stray. It says quite clearly that I'm not. PIP and RAY. PIP and RAY, it says on my tag. So *hands off*!

The café is closed when we walk past, but Phil is sitting at a table on his own, doing his accounts. This is it. This is it. Pip's going to do something. I just know it. We've got nowhere to stay and we might as well take our chance. But he just stands by the window, looking in. Well, I'm going to do something, then, I decide. I go to the door, jump up against it, and bark.

"Let us in!"

I can see Phil lift his head and then shake it. He goes back to his paperwork.

I try again. This time he notices Pip and gets up and unlocks the door.

"We're closed, I'm afraid," he says.

"Are you . . . Are you Phillip Seagrove?" Pip asks. I thought we *knew* he was Phillip Seagrove.

"Yes?" he answers inquiringly.

"I'm Pip Henderson."

Pip Henderson!

I thought *he* was Phillip Seagrove too. He told that farmer . . . And then it dawns on me how stupid I am. *Of course.* He just told the farmer the first name that popped into his head. And his head has been full of his dad.

Phil looks as if he ought to know who Pip Henderson is but can't quite recall.

Pip takes the photo out of his pocket and shows it to him. "This is you. Isn't it?"

Phil takes the picture and puts on his glasses.

"Yes! Where did you get this?"

"My mom gave it to me."

"Your mom? Who's your mom?"

"Janie. Janie Henderson . . ."

I can hear Pip faltering. *Please don't give up now,* I think. *You've gotten this far. You've got to keep going.*

"Janie Henderson! Your mom! My goodness, how is she? I haven't seen her in years! Where's she living now?"

"Mom's dead."

Phil's face sort of creases up.

"Oh, no," he says. "That's awful. How? How did she die?"

"Cancer."

And as he says that word Pip's shoulders begin to shake, and I look up and see two large tears rolling down his face and now his whole body is shaking and he is crying.

Phil puts his hand on Pip's shoulder. And then a strange look comes over his face. It is a mixture of concern and curiosity and fear.

"I'm so sorry," he says, guiding Pip into the café. "Come on in and sit down for a moment and you can tell me all about her."

Chapter 11

I sit under the table. For a moment, till Pip stops
crying, nothing is said. I lick his ankle so he
knows I'm still here and give him an encouraging
whimper.

I peek out and see Phil, standing by the counter,
the curious look still on his face.

"How old are you?" Phil asks.

"Fourteen."

And then there is a long silence and I can hear
everyone's hearts beating in their chests, including
mine, and I hear Phil whisper under his breath,
"Oh, my God!" and then he pulls back a chair
and sits down at the table.

Then I listen to them talking.

Talk. Talk.

Pip tells his dad things and Phil tells Pip things and they talk.

Talk. Talk. And now I'm thinking of Pip's mom. Janie. Janie. Jane. Now *there's* a familiar name. Who was Jane? And for some odd reason the picture of a crown pops into my head. But I can't think why.

I hear Phil call home and speak to his wife.

"I'm going to be a bit late back. Something extraordinary has happened. I'll tell you about it later. Is Sam all right?"

Then Phil's on the phone again. "Maisie? Can I have a word with your mom? No, it's not about the brownies. It's a lot more important than that!"

About twenty minutes later, a woman who looks like Maisie, but without the pink hair or the stud in the nose, gently knocks on the door.

"Sal!" Phil says. "Thanks for coming. I want you to meet someone special."

He puts his arm around Pip's shoulders.

"This is my—uh—son. Pip!"

My son Pip! I feel all warm and glowing. I want him to be my dad too.

I don't know Sal, but I can tell she's surprised.

"Does Viv know?" she says. "About Pip?" she adds, in case there might be some confusion.

"Well, yes . . . no . . . I haven't told her yet. It'll be a bit of a surprise. I didn't know, you see—about Pip. And so I need to talk everything through with her."

He hesitates for a moment.

"So—can you help me? I can't just walk in with Pip and say, 'This is my son.' Could you take him back with you tonight, so he has somewhere to stay? Then I'll have a chance to talk things over with Viv. I know this is a lot to ask. . . ."

Sal hesitates for a moment. Then says, "Yes—I can do that. Have you had any supper yet, Pip?"

Pip shakes his head. "Can Ray come too?"

"Who's Ray?"

"My dog, of course."

And I poke my head out from underneath the table and Sal laughs.

"Oh, yes!" she says, smiling for the first time. "He can certainly come."

"I'm a she," I tell her.

I'm glad that Sal is fine about me spending the night with Pip. I know he needs me more than ever tonight.

I've never slept on a bed as a dog before! It is *so* comfy, and I curl up in the crook of Pip's knees and he puts his hand on my head and whispers good night to me and I wonder if this will be our last night together because I have no idea what Viv will say.

In the morning, Maisie goes off to work at Café Zoo, and Pip and I hang around the kitchen while Sal cooks us breakfast. They are vegetarians, but she still manages a good breakfast. Grilled tomatoes, fried mushrooms, eggs, and vegetarian sausages. Because she wasn't expecting a dog to stay, there aren't any bone-shaped biscuits, so I get a couple of the sausages. Really, they are pretty good, considering that they don't have any meat in them.

The phone rings around nine o'clock and I hear Sal saying, "Yes. Yes. Really? Good. Yes. Yes. I'll do that. Good. OK. Bye!"

She turns to Pip.

"Phillip says he's going to shut the café early today and you can stay here while he works, as he's still sorting some stuff out. I'm supposed to take you there later on today."

Pip is looking nervous now. "Do you think it's going to be OK?"

Sal smiles at him. "I'm *sure* it's going to be OK. Now, there's a big jazz festival on in town today—people come for miles—so there'll be plenty to look at and listen to. Shall I show you the way to the beach so that you can walk Ray and then you can wander around town? Can you find your way back here about four o'clock, do you think?"

Pip nods. I think he's looking rather pale. He needs some fresh air and so do I. I've been here under the table for too long and I need to stretch my legs.

It's a blustery day outside. I'm sure it's going

to be good for Pip. Why shouldn't his dreams come true?

Sniff! Sniff! Seaweed, plastic bottles, beach shoes. I am assaulted by smells. My sense of smell has escalated and my hearing too. I can hear food hit a feeding bowl from more than twenty paces now. I can hear a baby cry in the next street. A couple argues. A car engine starts up. A tin can rattles along the sidewalk.

Hang on. Hang on.

Where's Pip now? Is he gone? Has he left me alone on the beach? But there he is—throwing pebbles into the water. How pleased I am to see him. As if I haven't seen him all day.

We wander back into town. There seem to be flags and bunting everywhere, and on almost every street corner there's a busker playing some instrument or other. On the green are a couple of tents, and people are cramming into them, trying to hear the music. I don't know why they bother— you can hear it perfectly well from out here.

Pip is not himself. He keeps sighing and looking at his watch. We sit down on the grass.

"I don't know, Ray," he says to me. "I don't think that this will work out. Why didn't he come and get us this morning and take us back to meet Viv? I bet they had a huge fight over it and Viv has threatened to leave if he brings us home, and he hasn't got the—the courage to tell us. I can't stand to hear him tell me we can't live with them. I think we should go. We might as well go, because he obviously doesn't want us."

I look at Pip and a huge tear rolls down his cheek. He sniffs and angrily wipes it away. I don't mind him crying, but I do mind him giving up hope.

"We've got to stay, Pip," I tell him. "If we go we'll never know and you'll spend your whole life wondering what might have happened."

I push up to his face and rub my wet nose against his cheek, and he lies back on the grass and looks at the sky. *The whole picture, Pip,* I think. *See the whole picture—don't worry about the missing pieces.*

I see a woman pushing a man in a wheelchair.

There is a golden dog at their side, wearing a coat with letters written on it. He looks smart.

"Sit, Dunbar!" I hear the woman say. She looks kind as well as anxious. She takes a locket out from around her neck and twists it through her fingers. Then she rests her hand on the man's shoulder and smiles at him. The man lifts his head and smiles back, and I suddenly feel all warm inside. I can't see the man's face now. He is sitting very still with his head bent again.

I'd like to have a yellow coat with letters written on it. Perhaps Pip will buy me a yellow coat with letters on it when it gets colder.

Pip has sat up and seen the dog too.

"Look, Ray! There's a dog wearing an Assistance Dog coat. I bet he's smart!" Then he bends down and gives me a hug.

'But not as smart as *you*! You're the best dog in the world. And if Dad's wife doesn't want us—well, I have *you*, and we'll find a way to get by."

I give him a big lick. I think he's putting on a brave face.

We walk near them, and the woman makes me think of hot buttered toast and warm baths and perfumed hugs and boiled eggs. I am feeling something, but I don't know what it is.

"What's up, Ray?" Pip asks.

But I don't answer him because I've got nothing to say.

The sad woman with the dog. The faceless man in the wheelchair. A boy on a bus. The house on — what street was it? I can only recall Marjorie's little house at the top of Barton Road. It's like they're all inside an hourglass and someone has tipped it upside down and they're slipping through to the bottom of the glass.

Going.

When we get back, Pip helps Sal make the brownies for the café and then it's four o'clock and time to go.

"It'll be all right, Pip," I tell him. "He seems like a nice man to have as a dad and he might give you a job in the café!"

Phil has already put the CLOSED sign up on the

door when we arrive, and I can see Maisie inside, wiping down the tables. Phil smiles at us and gives Pip a huge hug. This looks like a good sign to me. Maisie takes off her apron and, putting on her coat, gives us a wave.

"Bye, you guys! See you soon!"

We sit down at the table by the window again.

"Do you want a drink, Pip? Apple juice? Orange juice? I can make you a hot chocolate if you like," says Phil.

But Pip shakes his head. He just wants to *know*.

"You can imagine how surprised I was when you turned up, Pip," Phil starts saying. "I had no idea that Janie was pregnant. She didn't tell me, you know. She moved away as soon as college was over and never told me where she'd gone. I hope she managed all right. I'd hate to think of her struggling."

In between asking more questions about Pip's mom, he tells Pip about Viv and how, although shocked at first, she really wants to meet him. I watch Pip's foot sliding up and down the leg of his chair and I know he's still worried that Viv will not like him when she does finally get to meet him.

I can see a piece of toast that someone must have dropped under the next table and has escaped Maisie's sharp eye. I begin, very slowly, to edge myself toward it. Elbow. Elbow. Foot. Foot. Body. Mmmm.

There're some good smells coming from behind the counter too. I don't think anyone will notice if I go and check them out. Pip and his dad seem to have a lot to talk about.

There's a trash can and a bucket around the back of the counter. Scraps of bacon, toast, some omelet. All smelling pretty good. The trash can is too tall to get into, so I have to jump up. But it slips away from me and falls on my head.

"Aargh!" I say, and scuttle back to Pip's feet.

"Ray!" he says. "Bad dog! You can't do that!"

Bad dog? He's never called me *that* before. I'm a hungry dog, that's all. I suppose he doesn't want his dad to think I'm always going around knocking over trash cans.

I move from Pip's feet and sit under another table. They keep talking. Bad dog, indeed. I feel the corners of my mouth turn down and I sigh.

I'm not listening to them anymore. I'm just protecting Pip. I like his dad, and if he takes us in I'll be protecting him as well. And this Viv woman and Sam. I'd better brush up on my protecting skills. The snake man might walk into the café at any moment. I'm starting right now.

Then we're all up on our feet and going out of the café and down the street and back to the mauve house with the blue door. I have to check that our bicycle is still there, and it is. Pip seems to have forgotten about it. That's another thing I'll have to keep an eye out for.

I miss the introductions at the door because another dog has been at the gate. But there is Viv, a tall, smiling woman with dark hair, giving Pip a hug, and she smells of kindness and kisses and generosity.

"Hello!" she says to me. "Now, let's have a look at you. Ah, yes. You look like a good dog. You'll be nice to our Sam, won't you?"

And I know that, as long as he's not like Cyril, I'll take very good care of him.

We're in the house now. There seems to be a lot going on. Piles of books and newspapers. A bicycle in the hall. Paintings on the walls. Toys on the floor and, best of all, there is Sam. And he's my height! Small and fair-haired, he waddles toward me on his little chubby legs.

"Doggie!" he says, and he puts his arms around me and lays his head on my neck. I wag my tail, but ever so gently because I don't want to knock him over.

I don't sleep with Pip anymore. I have my own basket and my own rug — black and red checks. It is warm by the stove. I have my own bowl to eat out of and my own bowl to drink out of. Then there are Sam's toys and *my* toys, and sometimes Sam and I get a bit muddled and he's playing with my rubber chicken and I'm chewing on his toy duck. At night I lie awake, making sure nothing happens to anyone in the house — which is a *huge* responsibility, as there are so many of them. I am particularly protecting them from the snake man. I get my rest during the day, when I can see that everyone is OK and that no one has died in their sleep.

Pip works with Maisie at the café and sometimes I look after them all there and sometimes I look after Sam and Viv at home. And Pip takes me for walks on the beach. More often than not, Maisie comes too. I'm always pleased to see Maisie, with her smells of joy and laughter and hope.

And one day I saved Sam's life.

We were out on the sidewalk and Viv was talking to her neighbor and Sam had toddled off and was examining something in the middle of the road. I could hear something. I couldn't see it, but I could hear it. It was the engine of a car and it was being driven far too fast. *Screech. Scream. Roar.* It still hadn't come into view, but I sensed it. And this is what must be meant by having a sixth sense, because it was a very strong feeling and I just had to do something about it.

"Viv! Watch out for Sam!" I shouted, and I got hold of her skirt and I tugged it so that she would stop talking to her neighbor, and then I ran into the road and I pushed Sam with my nose to make him get up and I told him, in no uncertain terms, that he had to get out of the road *now*! Of course, he just giggled at me, even though he knew what I was saying. But Viv had seen. And now the car was coming around the bend on two wheels, and she ran into the road and scooped Sam up and we both raced back onto the sidewalk and the car tore past us and disappeared over the brow of the hill.

"Oh, Sam, you naughty boy!" she scolded him. "You must never go into the road."

And Sam started to cry, and I gave him a lick to tell him it was all right, really, but that his mom was right to get mad. And the neighbor gave me a pat and said, "I think this dog of yours saved his life with all that barking."

And Viv gave me a big hug.

Chapter 12

We are all around the table having a late breakfast.

I know there is someone there even before the doorbell rings. But Sam is feeding me some of his toast under the table, so I don't take much notice. Normally I'd be the first at the door, going, "Someone at the door! Come on—open up!" but today I don't want to leave this tasty morsel, so I let someone else go.

I hear a woman's voice. She sounds familiar.

"I'm so sorry to be a nuisance. Is this where the Seagroves live?"

"Yes," says Viv. "May I help you?"

"I just wondered if a lovely boy named Pip had managed to find your house and what had happened to him."

I practically choke on the toast in my hurry to get out from under the table and get to that door. There are a lot of legs in the way.

"Marjorie! Marjorie! It's me, Ray! Yes! We made it! We made it! Have you come back for your bicycle?"

"Oh," she says, bending down. "How lovely! Ray! You *did* find Pip's dad after all!"

I am so excited I have to go and tell Pip, but he's heard her voice too and is walking toward the door.

"Marjorie! You've come to see us!" Then I see a look of guilt pass over his face. "Oh, I should have told you! I'm so sorry—after all you did for us. I just didn't think! And Dad's told the authorities and it's all OK now and—oh, I'm so happy to see you!" Pip gives Marjorie a big hug, then, remembering his manners, he introduces her.

"Viv, Dad—this lady lives at your old house.

She saved us from food poisoning and gave us your address."

"And she lent us her bicycle," I add. Really, Pip seems to have forgotten all about that bicycle.

"You must come in!" says Phil with a big smile on his face. "I have a lot to thank you for."

"I brought you some letters I hadn't got around to forwarding on to you. In case," she added, "you didn't know what I was talking about."

Then they all go inside and sit around the table and I help clear the plates by giving them a lick, which I know I shouldn't, but they are busy talking and they haven't noticed me anyway.

Later I go and sit on the floor between Marjorie and Pip. Perhaps Marjorie could come and live here too. I'd really like that.

"Any time you want to go on vacation and you can't take Ray," she says, "I'm very happy to have her, you know. While you are away." I push my nose under her hand and give her a lick. I'm collecting quite a family now.

"Oh, by the way, Pip," Marjorie continues, "they caught the fellow who took my car. The police have been after him for ages. He was well known for stealing almost anything. In his photograph he looked like the most unpleasant man. And he had—you know—*tattoos*. He's locked up in prison now, thank goodness."

Locked up in prison? A huge sense of relief passes through my body. One less thing to worry about. Protecting everyone from the snake man was a very tiresome business.

Marjorie often visits us now. She particularly likes taking me for a walk when Viv goes out with Sam in the stroller. They all talk a lot. I don't listen much anymore. I don't understand most of it. There are words that are important, though, that I listen for. Words like *Let's go for a walk* and *Dinnertime, Ray!* And there are things that I would never do. Like I would never take a treat from anyone if they had asked me to leave it alone.

There are lots of people in my life now. Pip and his family and Maisie and Sal and Jack and Marjorie. I know we don't see Jack, but I still feel he's there. And I always keep a lookout for him. In case he's around the next corner or walking toward us along the road. Apart from Pip, who obviously is Number One, the person I like being with best is Sam. Little Sam with his laughter and tears. Sam who cannot talk yet. Well, not properly. He can say *Mom* and *Dad* and *Pip* and *doggie* and *toy* and *drinkie,* which is more than I can say.

And I know something about Sam that no one else does. I know that Sam understands me perfectly well.

I used to tell him things about myself and he knew what I was saying. And he would tell me things back. Like *No one understands me!* And *How long do I have to wait for my lunch?* And *Oh no, it's bath time again!* And all the time he gurgles and gabbles and makes funny noises, I understand him perfectly well too. But the curious thing is, the more he is able to speak the other humans' language, the less he is able to speak mine.

He's saying quite a lot now.

* * *

I'm sleeping more. When I dream, flashes of people I don't know come into my sleep. I don't dream about people I know.

There's a boy, sitting on a bus. He looks nice, but not as nice as Pip. He's there again, playing soccer. Then there is a man and a woman, a bit like Phil and Viv. In my dream I like them, but I don't know who they are. The woman is always cooking me meals and giving me hugs. Then there is a girl. I don't know who she is either, but she's nearly always in my dreams. I'd like to know her. She is friendly and kind, and in the dreams she is always *doing* things. In one dream she is flying a kite and I'm there too. Trying to fly the kite with her. And when it falls to the ground, we both laugh and we both run over and pick it up and try to fly it again.

Whenever I see Pip or Sam or Phil or Viv it's like I haven't seen them in a very long time. Particularly Pip. I'm always so pleased to set eyes on him. My sense of time has become very muddled now. For instance, it always seems like it should be time for a meal or a little snack.

The weather is warming up and Pip and Maisie

are sitting together on the sand and I'm standing by the edge of the sea. There's something really interesting half buried in the sand. I just have to go and unearth it.

Yes! I thought so. A piece of wood.

I pick it up and run over to Pip, dropping it by his side. He ruffles my ears but makes no attempt to get up and throw it for me. I take it around to Maisie, but all she does is play with the wood and idly bury it again by her side. I go back to the sea. *Splash, splash,* the water is swirling around my legs. Warm and silky.

I look across the horizon. I walk a little farther into the water. I look behind me. Pip and Maisie are still sitting in the sand, chatting away. I start to swim. I can hear, just faintly, above the lapping of the waves and the seagulls screaming by the cliffs, a voice. Calling me.

"Daisy! Daisy! Come in now!"

I am swimming into the waves and I think of Pip on his birthday when he said it was like going back into the womb. The water is warm and there is a voice again. Calling. Calling.

A wave washes over me and there is my room on Alexander Avenue with the mattress on the floor and the SAVE THE PLANET posters on the walls, and the water now is all pink and swirly like my mosquito net. And there is Jessica Warner and Owen Taylor and Ms. Roberts, the gym teacher, all waving at me.

They're all out there. Mom and Dad and Jack too. And it's Mom's voice I can hear.

"Daisy! Daisy! Come in! The water's really warm!"

Another wave splashes over my head.

Then I'm in the car with Dad. And Mom is at the door calling to us, in her I'M THE BOSS apron. "Don't forget to buy some cheese biscuits!" And we're out on the road now. And Dad turns to me and says, "Could you just check that my wallet's on the backseat, Daisy?" And I unbuckle my seat belt and turn to look and there's the wallet. Brown and worn, with my scarf and Dad's hat. And I turn back and something huge and black blots out the light. It is a horse jumping over the hedge. I look in wonder as it clears the hedge and I hear Dad shouting and I see fear in the horse's eyes.

And then there's a noise like crashing, crumpling metal, and everywhere are diamonds catching the light. Diamonds in my hair and in my face and I'm flying now.

Weightless.

Nothing.

Dark. Empty nothing.

Crashing. Crashing.

It is waves crashing around my head.

Turn around. Swim back to shore. Look around.

There he is.

Walking toward me. Along the beach.

Calling my name.

"Ray! Ray!"

Ears. Bark. Tail wag.

Run.

Stop.

Happy. Happy. Happy. My Pip.

Here.

Acknowledgments

The Dog, Ray brought my agent, Suzy Jenvey, and me together. All thanks to her for believing in it from the very beginning. Also Emma Matthewson, my lovely editor, and all at Hot Key who have helped Ray to finally wag her tail on the page. Huge thanks to Elinor Bagenal, who encouraged me so much with the writing of it and who put me in touch with Suzy. Also Serita Lewis, whose amazing photographs of people living on the streets were truly informative; her knowledge — and that of some *Big Issue* sellers — helped me with writing about Pip and

Jack. Johnny Bull and Susie Alexander, for reading it before anyone else and helping me with ideas and improvements. And finally to our own dog, Beezle, who was the inspiration. He let me into the ways of dogs.